What's the only thing scarier than the creepy old neighbor's house? The creepy old neighbor . . .

Amanda grabbed the ball and took off, running fast enough to break Olympic records. She only looked back once. No one was behind her. Ahead of her was the fence. She could see the amazement on her friends' faces. Just a few more feet, and Amanda was home free!

"Move!" Amanda yelled as she hit the fence hard. "Get out of the way!"

Jarrad, Kevin, and Laura stepped back to make room for Amanda to squeeze through. As she began to, they were already congratulating her, sure that it was over, and that she was safe.

Amanda was pretty sure of it too. But she was wrong. Because Amanda was only halfway through the fence when she felt icy, skeletal fingers clamp down onto her wrist.

STARSCAPE BOOKS BY ANNETTE CASCONE AND GINA CASCONE

DEADTIME STORIES™

Grave Secrets

The Witching Game

The Beast of Baskerville

Invasion of the Appleheads

Little Magic Shop of Horrors

Grandpa's Monster Movies

GRAVE SECRETS

ANNETTE CASCONE and GINA CASCONE

A TOM DOHERTY ASSOCIATES BOOK • NEW YORK

A Starscape Book
Published by Tom Doherty Associates, LLC
175 Fifth Avenue
New York, NY 10010

www.tor-forge.com

The Library of Congress has cataloged the hardcover edition as follows:

Cascone, Annette.
    Grave secrets / Annette Cascone and Gina Cascone.—1st ed.
        p. cm.
    ISBN 978-0-7653-3065-9 (hardcover)
    ISBN 978-1-4299-9291-6 (e-book)
1. Horror tales. 2. Old age—Fiction. 3. Ghosts—Fiction. 4. Horror stories. I. Title.
    PZ7.C26673 Gre 2012
    813.6—dc23

                                                                        2011287623

ISBN 978-0-7653-3071-0 (trade paperback)

Starscape books may be purchased for educational, business, or promotional use. For information on bulk purchases, please contact Macmillan Corporate and Premium Sales Department at 1-800-221-7945, extension 5442, or write specialmarkets@macmillan.com.

First Edition: January 2012
First Trade Paperback Edition: May 2014

Printed in in the United States of America

0 9 8 7 6 5 4 3 2 1

For Elise,

the baby sister we look up to

GRAVE SECRETS

1

There was no stopping what was about to happen. And Amanda Peterson knew it. Even as she watched Jarrad Clark and Kevin Stewart racing toward the back of the yard, she knew it was hopeless.

"No!" Laura Baxter screamed. But it was already too late.

The ball game was over. Amanda had hit a home run. Only nobody cheered. And Amanda didn't run the bases, or do a victory dance, or even smile. She just stood frozen, watching in horror as the ball sailed over her back fence into the yard of the house that stood at 704 Shadow Lane.

"I'm out of here," Laura announced, dropping her glove

and heading past Amanda toward the gate. Laura always bugged out at the first sign of trouble.

"Oh, no you don't!" Amanda caught Laura by the back of her shirt as she tried to escape.

"I am not going over there to get that ball," Laura said, shaking her head adamantly. "I don't care what you say. I'm not doing it. So don't even ask me."

Like anybody would. Cool, calm, and collected were not adjectives that applied to Laura in any situation. Even momentary discomfort was too much for her to bear. That was why Laura walked around with only one ear pierced. She told everybody it was a fashion statement. But Amanda knew the truth. Because Amanda was there when it happened. The first pinch of the piercing gun sent Laura into hysterics. And she practically destroyed the whole Piercing Pagoda trying to escape. Laura was definitely not the kind of person you sent on a life-or-death mission.

"I wasn't going to ask you to go," Amanda assured her. "I'm gonna go. I just don't want you to leave me all by myself in case something terrible happens." Amanda released her grip on Laura. "I wouldn't leave you," she added deliberately. Then she turned and headed for the back fence. Laura followed a moment later, just as Amanda knew she would.

Jarrad and Kevin were peering intently through the gap where a section of the Petersons' fence had come loose from the post. "It's not good," Jarrad said gravely as he stepped back so that Amanda could see for herself.

Peeking through the crack in the fence was like peeking through a crack in time. The property at 704 Shadow Lane was so strange and eerie that it seemed like a horrible hallucination. Even in the middle of the day, it was dark there. The enormous old trees in the back of the yard blocked out the sun completely. And the ancient gray stone house loomed in the shadows, gloomy and foreboding. All of the windows were hung with heavy draperies that were always closed. Except the basement windows, which were covered with grime and thick iron bars. It was easy to imagine that it wasn't a basement at all, but a dungeon. The only thing scarier than the house at 704 Shadow Lane was the old woman who lived inside it.

"Over there." Kevin pointed out where Amanda's ball had landed. "Right next to the shed where she throws the rats after she bites their heads off."

Amanda shuddered. It was just one of the many rumors about old Mrs. Barns. And while Amanda didn't want to believe that it was true, she knew enough about Mrs. Barns to be afraid that it just might be.

"If I were you," Jarrad said, "I'd forget about going in there after that ball."

"She can't do that," Laura shrieked, horrified by the suggestion. "What if Barnsey gets her evil old hands on it? What happens then? Huh?"

"Probably the same thing that happened to that Lizard kid," Kevin answered.

"What lizard kid?" Jarrad asked.

"The Lizard kid," Kevin repeated impatiently. "You know, the kid that blew up on his own front yard."

It was an old story that had been handed down so many times that there was no one around who had actually seen it happen. But all the kids still believed that it had.

"Lu-zard," Jarrad corrected him.

"Lizard, Lu-zard, who cares what his name is." Kevin rolled his eyes in exasperation. "The kid's still dead, isn't he? And all because Barnsey got her hands on something that belonged to him."

It was a water pistol. At least that's the way Amanda had heard it. And while there were several other variations of the story, one thing was certain. There really was a Frederick Luzard. And he really was dead. They'd seen his headstone in the cemetery. He was eleven and a half years old when he died, the same age as Amanda.

"Nobody really knows what happened to that kid," Jarrad said, trying to be the voice of reason.

"Cut me a break." Kevin was not about to drop the subject. He was scared to death of Mrs. Barns and took every opportunity to spread the fear around. "Everybody knows what happened to that kid. He burned up just like that!" Kevin snapped his fingers. "Barnsey put a spell on him. And the kid fried."

"It's too awful to even think about." Laura cringed.

"Yeah, well, think about what she did to Todd French!"

Todd French was the only person they actually knew who claimed to have suffered under an evil spell cast on him by Mrs. Barns. It all started the day after one of his brothers tossed his baseball cap onto Barnsey's property to see if Todd was brave enough to go and get it. But he didn't go get it. And according to Todd, it was the worst decision of his entire life.

"Barnsey did not put a spell on Todd French," Jarrad insisted.

"Oh, yeah," Kevin shot back. "Then how do you explain the twenty-seven stitches he got in his head the day after Barnsey got his cap?"

"It was nine," Jarrad corrected him. "And he walked into the sliding doors at the supermarket."

"Because Barnsey made him," Kevin insisted. "And a week later, she made like six of his teeth fall out."

"No, the dentist had to *pull* two of his molars out to make room for all the rest of those buck teeth he's got."

"And what about the bed bugs?" Kevin asked.

Amanda was waiting for the logical explanation. But even Jarrad seemed to be stumped by the bed bugs.

"Todd French does not have a spell on him," Jarrad finally huffed. "Besides, he's still alive, isn't he?"

"For now," Kevin said ominously, looking directly at Amanda.

"You can't let Barnsey get her hands on that ball." Laura pointed out what Amanda already knew.

Amanda wasn't entirely convinced that Todd French was suffering at the hands of Mrs. Barns. But she didn't want to take any chances, either. "I've got to go get it," Amanda announced. And before she could change her mind, she started to squeeze through the fence.

"No." Jarrad stopped her. "I'll go."

"Yeah." Laura jumped on the offer. "Let Jarrad go. He can run faster than anybody."

Amanda really wanted to let Jarrad go in her place. But she couldn't. If Jarrad messed up and Barnsey got her hands on that ball, Amanda would be the one to fry for it anyway. "I've got to do it," Amanda told him. "It's my ball."

She could tell by the look on Jarrad's face that he was relieved she'd let him off the hook. Amanda knew Jarrad would have gone in her place if she asked him to. He was always trying to prove to the rest of them that they didn't have to be so scared of Barnsey. But deep down, she was sure that Jarrad was every bit as scared as she was.

"Just don't let her catch you," Kevin warned, "or you'll end up in her dungeon with that other little girl."

The dungeon was Barnsey's basement. It was where she tortured all of her victims—before she finally buried them.

"Why don't you just shut up?" Jarrad backhanded Kevin. "There is no little girl."

"Is too," Kevin insisted. "I know someone who saw her."

"Oh, really," Jarrad said. "Who?"

"Todd French," Kevin answered.

"Again with Todd French?" Jarrad was exasperated. "Todd French can't even see his own two feet in front of him. Why do you think he has to wear those goggle glasses to school?"

"Well, he saw the little girl," Kevin declared. "And he said that she was all bloody and stuff."

Amanda could see the panic on Laura's face as she turned back toward the fence. If Amanda was going to do this, she had to do it now, before she chickened out.

"Keep your fingers crossed," Amanda told the rest of them. "And watch out for Barnsey. If she sees me, I'm dead."

Amanda took a deep breath. As she squeezed through the gap in the fence, she could feel her heart pounding all the way down to her fingertips. She focused her eyes on the ball. *Not so far away*, she told herself. Amanda was a fast runner, almost as fast as Jarrad. She could be there and back in less than a minute. It was going to be okay. She'd make it just fine.

"Go," Jarrad urged her, peeking through the gap from the safe side of the fence. "Fast!"

As Amanda tore off, she heard Kevin calling after her. "Watch out for the rats!"

Rats! She'd forgotten all about the rats! But there was no stopping now. Besides, rats—even ones without their heads—were a whole lot less terrifying to Amanda than the thought of Barnsey getting her hands on that ball. Still, she watched the ground carefully, praying that she wouldn't step on anything—dead or alive.

Amanda made it to the shed. The ball was lying right near the open door, and there were no headless rats piled around it. But as she bent down to grab the ball, she heard something moving around inside the shed.

Amanda's heart stopped. What if the rats were in there?

Or worse yet, what if it was Barnsey? What if Barnsey was waiting to grab her and take her to the dungeon with the other little girl?

Amanda grabbed the ball and took off, running fast enough to break Olympic records. She looked back only once. No one was behind her. Ahead of her, and closing fast, was the fence. She could see the amazement on her friends' faces. Just a few more feet, and Amanda was home free.

"Move!" Amanda ordered the rest of them as she hit the fence hard. "Get out of the way!"

Jarrad, Kevin, and Laura stepped back to make room for Amanda to squeeze through.

"You did it." Laura congratulated.

"I can't believe it!" Kevin chimed in. "You made it!"

But Amanda was only halfway through the fence when she felt icy, skeletal fingers clamp down on to her wrist, as cold and as inescapable as handcuffs.

2

N ooooooooo!!!!"

Amanda screamed as she felt the bony fingers tighten around her wrist, practically crushing it.

She was halfway back into the safety of her own yard! But now she wasn't going to make it the rest of the way!

"Where do you think you're going?" Barnsey's voice croaked.

"Help me!" Amanda shouted frantically at her friends. "Don't let her take me to the dungeon!"

Jarrad had already grabbed her other arm and was pulling as hard as he could without hurting her. Kevin grabbed on to Jarrad and started pulling him. And Laura grabbed on to Kevin. It was like a giant tug-of-war. But even though Barnsey was outnumbered, she was still winning. For a scrawny old woman, she seemed to have superhuman strength. Because Barnsey was holding Amanda in a death grip from which there seemed to be no escape.

"Oh, I don't think I'll bring you to the dungeon," Barnsey cackled. "Maybe I'll just drag you over to the shed and bite *your* head off!"

They all shrieked in terror as they struggled frantically to pull Amanda free. As they tugged with every ounce of strength that each one of them could muster, Barnsey suddenly released Amanda's wrist. The four of them toppled over like dominoes. But they'd barely touched the ground before they were up and running. And they didn't stop until they hit the back door of Amanda's house. Only then did they turn to look behind them.

Luckily, Barnsey hadn't followed them. She wasn't even watching through the fence.

"That was a close call," Jarrad gasped, doubling over to catch his breath.

"Way too close," Kevin agreed.

"I thought I was a goner." Amanda had to struggle to

hold back tears. She had never been so terrified in her life. It had barely sunk in that it was over and she was safe.

"How did Barnsey get you?" Laura asked. "Didn't you see her out there?"

"Didn't you?" Amanda shot back. "You guys were supposed to be looking out for me."

"We were," Jarrad assured her. "But I never saw her coming."

"Me neither." Kevin backed him up. "It's like she appeared out of nowhere."

"It's because she's a witch," Laura said. "She's got all kinds of evil powers we don't even know about."

"She does not." Jarrad tried to stop that conversation from starting all over again.

"Then how did she just appear like that?" Amanda demanded.

"I don't know." Jarrad shook his head in frustration. "Maybe she was there all the time and we just didn't see her because she was hiding behind a tree. There are lots of trees back there big enough for her to hide behind." Jarrad always had a logical explanation for everything.

"Maybe." Amanda shrugged. She wished she could

believe that Jarrad was right about Barnsey. But after what had just happened, it was getting more difficult.

"Besides," Jarrad continued, "what difference does it make now? You got the ball, and you made it back in one piece."

Amanda hadn't even thought about that. She looked at the baseball in her hand and laughed in relief. But when she tried to toss it up into the air, her fingers wouldn't let go. She'd been clutching it so hard, for so long, that her fingers had gone a little bit numb.

Jarrad gently pried it from her hand. "You're pretty brave," he told her.

"Not really," Amanda admitted. "I was scared to death the whole time. Especially when Barnsey grabbed me." Amanda rubbed her wrist, trying to forget what Barnsey's fingers felt like wrapped around it. Then, her heart started to pound. "Oh no!" Amanda cried.

"What is it?" Laura asked, her nerves still on edge.

"My bracelet!" Amanda held out the wrist she'd been rubbing. "It's gone! I've lost my bracelet!"

"Your friendship bracelet?" Laura touched her own bracelet, the one that matched Amanda's. "Are you sure?"

"It's gone." Amanda's voice rose in dismay.

"Are you sure you were wearing it?" Jarrad tried to keep her calm.

Amanda nodded, looking terrified. "What if I lost it in Barnsey's yard? Or what if she ripped it right off my wrist while she was holding on to me?"

"Oh, man," Kevin said, staring wide-eyed at Amanda. "If Barnsey's got your bracelet, you're doomed!"

"Shut up, Kevin," Jarrad warned. "You probably just lost it while we were playing ball," he said to Amanda. "I bet it's right here in your own yard."

Jarrad didn't wait for anybody to agree or disagree with him. He just started looking for the bracelet.

The rest of them followed his lead. There was nothing else they could do.

The grass was long, too long to be able to spot something as small as a bracelet easily. So they got on their hands and knees and combed the lawn carefully, inch by inch.

Amanda prayed that Jarrad was right, that if they searched long enough and hard enough, they would find her bracelet. *Think positive,* she told herself as she ran her fingers through the grass.

Amanda's face was so close to the ground, she didn't see what was ahead of her . . . until she crept forward and found herself face-to-face with something so awful, the scream stuck in her throat, and when she opened her mouth, no sound escaped at all.

3

When Amanda finally managed to scream, it was loud and shrill, and seemed to go on forever. And before she finally ran out of air, her friends were beside her.

Laura gasped the moment she saw what Amanda was screaming about.

"Oh, gross," Jarrad groaned as he pulled Amanda to her feet.

Kevin didn't flinch. In fact, he bent down to take a closer look. "This guy's been dead for a while," he announced, nudging the dead squirrel with the toe of his sneaker. "He's already got like riga-morphasis and all. You see?" Kevin nudged the squirrel again. "He's hard as a rock."

"It's *rigor mortis*, you idiot," Jarrad corrected him. "And I don't wanna see."

"Poor little guy," Amanda said, brushing herself off. "What do you think happened to him?"

"I don't know," Jarrad told her. "Maybe he was just old."

"Or maybe he fell out of a tree." Laura offered her own explanation.

"Squirrels don't just fall out of trees," Kevin said.

"Oh, yeah?" Laura shot back. "Well, maybe this one did."

"Or maybe somebody killed him," Kevin suggested ominously.

Laura laughed. "That's so stupid," she told Kevin. "Who would kill a squirrel?"

Kevin turned his head to look at Barnsey's house. And Laura stopped laughing immediately.

"Cut it out, Kevin," Jarrad scolded before Kevin could open his mouth. "Barnsey did not kill this squirrel."

"Oh, yeah?" Kevin opened it anyway. "Well, maybe she did!"

"For what?" Jarrad asked impatiently.

"Yeah," Laura chimed in nervously. "For what?"

"I don't know," Kevin said. "Maybe she was gonna eat him or something."

"Everybody knows she eats rats," Laura reminded him. "Not squirrels."

"Yeah, well, maybe she's sick of rats," Kevin went on. "I mean how many rats can a person eat? Or maybe she was just gonna have him for dessert."

"Oh, brother," Jarrad huffed. "If Barnsey wanted to eat this squirrel, what's he doing over here?"

Amanda didn't believe for a second that Barnsey was going to eat the squirrel for dessert. Or even for dinner, for that matter. In fact, she was beginning to think the whole conversation was pretty funny. Until Kevin finally spit out his response.

"Maybe she threw him over here to send us a message," Kevin told them.

"What kind of message?" Laura asked, wide-eyed.

"A bad one," Kevin answered. "Like if she catches us in her yard again, we're gonna end up just like him!" Kevin pointed at the dead squirrel.

"There's something seriously wrong with you," Jarrad told Kevin, exasperated. "The poor little thing just died back here, that's all. Mrs. Barns did not kill him. And she is not trying to send us a message."

Amanda wanted to believe that with all her heart. Only problem was, Mrs. Barns really had threatened to drag Amanda to the shed and bite her head off. So maybe Kevin wasn't as crazy as Jarrad thought he was.

"Yeah, well, I'd be praying really hard that we find your bracelet on this side of the fence," Kevin told Amanda. "Because Barnsey doesn't even have to catch you to kill you!"

Laura went pale. And so did Amanda.

"Are you just stupid?" Jarrad asked Kevin. "Or are you a *real* moron? Mrs. Barns has never killed anybody. And she's not going to, either!"

"Oh, yeah?" Kevin shot back. "Why don't you try telling that to the Lizard kid!"

"Just shut up, Kevin!" Amanda finally snapped. Kevin was working her into such a terrified state that she just couldn't take it anymore.

Jarrad was right. Mrs. Barns hadn't killed anybody. And she wasn't going to, either. At least that's what Amanda told herself. And as she tried to calm her fears, Amanda also told herself that she had to have lost her bracelet while they were playing ball. Yeah. The bracelet was definitely somewhere in her own backyard. And sooner or later it would turn up. She was sure of it. Well . . . almost sure of it.

"Yeah, Kevin," Jarrad said, agreeing with Amanda. "Why don't you just shut up."

"Fine," Kevin huffed. "My lips are sealed." Kevin turned the imaginary key to lock his lips shut. But he wasn't silent for even a second before he had to add another two cents. "Just like his!" Kevin nudged the dead squirrel with his foot again.

Amanda shook her head at him in disgust.

"So what do you wanna do with him?" Jarrad asked Amanda as he backhanded Kevin in the arm.

"I guess we should bury him," Amanda answered, with what she thought to be the only answer.

But Kevin couldn't resist offering another. "I say we chuck him back onto Barnsey's yard."

"That's mean," Laura told him. "This poor little squirrel doesn't deserve that. Even if Barnsey really did chuck him over here."

"We're gonna bury him," Jarrad insisted, before another Barnsey conversation could begin. "It's the right thing to do."

Amanda sent Laura into the garage to get a shovel, while she ran into the house to find a shoe box big enough to hold the body. By the time the two of them returned with the shovel and squirrel coffin in hand, Kevin and Jarrad were in the back of the yard, looking for an appropriate burial plot.

"How about we put him here?" Jarrad suggested, stepping on a piece of ground about a foot from the fence.

"No," Amanda told him. "That's too close to Ralph." Ralph was Amanda's pet hamster. But he wasn't Amanda's pet for long. Two weeks after Amanda got him, Ralph had died. "See," Amanda pointed to a rock next to Jarrad's foot. "That's his headstone." The stone was all covered with dirt, but the name "Ralph" was definitely still visible.

"How about here?" Jarrad stepped on another spot.

Amanda shook her head. "I think Herman is there."

"Who's Herman?" Laura asked.

"The goldfish," Amanda reminded her. "Remember?"

"Oh, yeah." Laura nodded.

"While you guys are picking out a plot," Kevin said impatiently, "why don't you give me the coffin and I'll go get the diseased."

"*Deceased*, you imbecile," Jarrad corrected him.

"Whatever." Kevin grabbed the shoe box from Amanda and headed for the squirrel.

It took at least another fifteen minutes to find a spot by the fence in the "pet cemetery" that wasn't occupied. But when they finally moved past Snitch the canary's grave, Jarrad grabbed the shovel and started to dig.

The ground was pretty hard, and Amanda could see that Jarrad was having a difficult time digging up the dirt. The shovel kept hitting one stone after another. As Amanda stood there watching him, she hoped she hadn't picked a cemetery plot that was already being used by another dearly departed pet she'd forgotten about. In fact, Amanda was hoping that the shovel wouldn't hit anything else at all.

But it did—and Amanda's heart came to a complete and total stop.

From under the earth where Jarrad was digging came a faint, muffled sound. It wasn't just a sound, Amanda realized with alarm. It was a voice. A voice that cried "*Ma-ma!*"

There was definitely a grave under their feet . . . and Amanda was pretty sure it wasn't a pet's.

4

Did you hear that?" Amanda practically whispered. She was quiet because she wanted to hear the sound if it came again.

"It sounded like a baby," Laura said nervously.

"Yeah, well, you'd better hope it's not a baby," Kevin told her. "Because that sound came from that hole. And if it's a baby, then somebody buried it back here."

"It's not a baby," Jarrad assured them. "Who would bury a baby in Amanda's backyard?"

Kevin started to answer.

But Jarrad cut him off. "Don't even say Barnsey."

"Well, if it's not a baby, then what is it?" Laura asked.

"I don't know. But I'm gonna find out." Jarrad lifted the shovel and was about to drive it into the ground again.

"Don't!" Amanda stopped him. "What if it *is* a baby?"

"It's not a baby!" Jarrad shouted. But he dropped the shovel anyway and got down on his knees to dig with his hands.

Kevin joined in. But Amanda and Laura stood back.

"What is it?" Amanda demanded, the second Jarrad stopped digging. She didn't want to see for herself. Not yet. Not until she was sure it wasn't something awful. She'd already had more than enough scares for one day.

"It's just a stupid doll," Kevin answered, sounding disappointed. He tossed it out of the hole, and it landed right at Amanda's feet.

Amanda and Laura bent down to inspect the doll more closely while Jarrad and Kevin continued the work of burying the squirrel.

"It sure is ugly," Laura said.

Amanda was forced to agree. If the doll had ever been pretty, she showed no signs of it now. Her clothes were filthy, and tattered, and worm-eaten. The hair was all matted, and stuck straight up from the top of her head.

Amanda could tell that it used to be blond, but now it was mostly muddy brown. The doll's face was dirty and scratched. One blue eye was open, and the other was caked shut with dirt. It was obvious that the doll had been in the ground a long, long time.

"Where do you suppose she came from?" Amanda asked.

"From in the hole," Kevin said over his shoulder as he put the squirrel coffin in where the doll had been.

"I mean, who put it there?" Amanda rolled her eyes.

"Didn't you?" Laura asked.

"No," Amanda told her. "I'd never bury one of my dolls." It seemed like a creepy thing to do, kind of like burying a person.

It had been a long time since Amanda had actually played with dolls, although she did have an enormous collection of them. They were fine porcelain dolls that Amanda's mother began collecting for her from the time she was born. By the time she was ten, Amanda had so many dolls that her father had to build extra shelves above her bed so she could display all of them.

"Maybe Robin did it," Jarrad suggested, as he began to cover the squirrel coffin with dirt.

Robin was Amanda's little sister. She was only five years old and she still liked to play with dolls. Only she didn't play with them very nicely. Robin didn't own a single doll that still had all its body parts. She'd colored on them, tattooed them, and butchered their hair with her safety scissors. It was entirely possible that Robin played funeral with them as well.

Amanda picked the doll up off the ground. She held it with two fingers, and looked it over closely. She wanted to make sure that there were no bugs on it; no slugs, or centipedes. When she was satisfied that there weren't, she started brushing off the dirt.

"No way Robin buried this," she told the rest of them. "Look at it. This doll is really, really old. Whoever buried it did it a long, long time ago."

"Maybe it was the people who lived here before you," Kevin suggested.

"Nobody lived here before us," Amanda reminded him. "We moved into this house when it was brand-new. This whole backyard was nothing but woods before our house was built."

"That means somebody buried this doll in the woods," Laura said. "Now that's *really* creepy."

"What's so creepy about it?" Jarrad laughed. "It's just a stupid doll."

But there *was* something creepy about it. At least Amanda thought there was. Only she couldn't figure out what it was about the doll that was bothering her so much.

Until Jarrad pointed it out. "You're just weirded out because it said 'Mama.'"

That was it. That was exactly what was troubling Amanda. She squeezed the cloth body in her hands, feeling around, hoping she'd find what she was looking for. But she didn't.

A chill ran up Amanda's spine. "How did this doll say 'Mama'?" she asked her friends, knowing that even Jarrad would not have a logical explanation after he heard what she said next. "It doesn't have a voice box!"

5

"Gimme that thing," Kevin said, grabbing the doll from Amanda's hands. First he looked it over. Then he squeezed it a couple of times. Then he banged it against his leg. But no sound came from the doll.

"See," Amanda said. "I told you it doesn't have a voice box!"

Laura's eyes were wide with fear. "Then how did it say 'Mama'?"

"Maybe it's haunted," Kevin shrieked, dropping the doll onto the ground.

Amanda knew that Kevin was just trying to scare them,

and she didn't appreciate it one bit. She was already scared half to death. "Knock it off," she shouted at Kevin.

Kevin burst out laughing. "Gotcha!"

"You don't really think this doll is haunted, do you?" Jarrad asked Amanda as he dumped the last shovelful of dirt on top of the squirrel's grave.

That was exactly what Amanda thought. What else was there to think? "It doesn't have a voice box," Amanda repeated, speaking very slowly, as if Jarrad were a complete idiot.

"The voice box must have fallen out in the hole," Jarrad replied, speaking to Amanda as if she were an even bigger idiot.

Amanda felt pretty stupid as she bent down to pick up the doll.

"You guys are such suckers," Kevin taunted.

"And you're a real jerk," Laura shot back. "Besides, I still think that doll is pretty creepy."

Amanda was about to agree when her mother appeared at the back door of the house to call her in for dinner.

As her friends left the yard through the side gate, Amanda headed across the patio toward the house with the doll still in her hands. She thought about bringing it inside to show it to her parents, but then she decided that probably wasn't a very good idea. Her mother would only yell at her for bringing something that dirty into the house. So she set the doll down on the picnic table before she went in.

Amanda realized she'd made the right decision the minute she started telling her parents about the doll.

"Please tell me you didn't bring that thing into the house," her mother said as she sat down at the dinner table.

"No," Amanda assured her. "I left her outside on the picnic table."

Her mother made a face as if that were almost as bad.

"I wanna see her." Amanda's little sister, Robin, hopped up from the table and started out of the room.

Amanda's father stuck out his arm and caught Robin before she could make it past him. "Oh no, you don't," he laughed. "It's dinnertime, pal."

Robin plunked herself back down in her seat.

"So what are you planning to do with this doll?" Amanda's mother asked.

"I don't know." Amanda shrugged. "She's in pretty bad shape."

"Maybe you ought to just throw her in the trash," her mother suggested hopefully.

Amanda knew that was probably what she would end up doing. But somehow that seemed even worse than burying her. "Don't you think it's weird that someone buried a doll on our property?" Amanda asked her parents.

"Well, it hasn't always been our property," Amanda's father pointed out.

"I know," Amanda told him. "It wasn't anybody's property before we moved in. It was just woods."

"It was all just woods," her father agreed. "But some of the property actually belonged to Mrs. Barns."

"Mrs. Barns?" Amanda gasped. That was the last thing she needed to hear.

"Yes," her father said with a chuckle. "Mrs. Barns. Don't you remember what happened when we put up the fence?"

Amanda shook her head no.

"Sure you do," her father said. "It was a terrible mess. The guys who put up the fence built it two feet back over our property line, right onto Mrs. Barns's backyard. And we would have had to move the whole thing if Mrs. Barns hadn't been so nice about it. Luckily, she just offered to sell us the last couple of feet of her property so that we could leave the fence right where it was."

"So the doll we dug up wasn't really buried in our backyard at all?" Amanda asked with alarm. "It was buried in Barnsey's backyard?"

"Amanda," her mother reprimanded. "How many times have I told you not to call Mrs. Barns that? It's not nice."

Amanda was too upset to even pretend to be sorry.

"Does it really make a difference whose backyard the doll was buried in?" Amanda's father asked.

Amanda knew that if she answered that question honestly, she'd just be in for another lecture about "poor old Mrs. Barns." So Amanda simply shrugged, without saying another word.

Amanda's parents thought that all the stories about Mrs. Barns were nothing but nonsense. They insisted that Mrs. Barns was so tormented by the neighborhood kids that she only pretended to be mean and scary so that she could keep the constant harassment at a safe distance. They even felt sorry for Mrs. Barns. They said that she was probably just "lonely" because she didn't have any family or friends. They were sure that if the kids would just stop telling stories about her and spend some time trying to get to know her better, they'd find out that Mrs. Barns was just a "sweet little old lady."

Kevin had tried to convince Amanda's parents that maybe the reason Mrs. Barns was "lonely" was because she'd *buried* her family and friends in her backyard—after she'd tortured them in her dungeon. But Mr. and Mrs. Peterson didn't want to hear about it. And they definitely didn't want Amanda repeating it, particularly in front of Robin.

Still, Amanda couldn't help wondering if maybe Kevin was right, especially now.

Maybe Barnsey's family and friends aren't buried in her backyard! Amanda thought with a gulp. *Maybe they're buried in mine!*

The idea hit Amanda so hard, she nearly choked on her chicken.

"Amanda," her mother reacted. "Are you okay?"

Amanda nodded yes, while her brain kept screaming no.

"Here," Mr. Peterson said, handing Amanda her glass. "Take a sip of water."

Amanda did as she was told. But it wasn't a piece of chicken sliding down the wrong pipe that had Amanda gasping for air. It was Barnsey.

She didn't say so, but the answer to her father's question was "yes." Digging up that doll from Barnsey's backyard did make a difference—all the difference in the world.

6

By the time Amanda went to bed, she had worked herself into such a state that she couldn't possibly fall asleep. Lying there in the dark, quiet room, with nothing to distract her, Amanda's imagination began to run wild about Barnsey, and the doll, and her lost bracelet, and the dead squirrel. And while she tried to convince herself that Kevin was wrong about Mrs. Barns and that her parents were right, Kevin's ideas were starting to seem less and less crazy by the minute.

Sweet little old ladies don't threaten to drag you behind a shed and bite your head off, Amanda reminded herself. Mrs. Barns was not pretending to be mean and scary. She really was! And no matter how hard she tried, Amanda couldn't seem to convince herself otherwise. She only hoped that Mrs. Barns wasn't as evil, and as powerful, as Kevin thought she was. Because if Mrs. Barns really was a witch, if she really did have the power to put spells on people, Amanda might be in big, big trouble. Especially if Mrs. Barns really did have her bracelet!

That thought hit Amanda so hard, it practically knocked the wind right out of her. As she pulled the covers more tightly around her, she pictured Barnsey down in her dungeon conjuring up some horrible fate for her.

"Stop it," Amanda said out loud, trying to force the image from her brain. "Just stop it!"

Suddenly, the sound of another voice distracted her.

Amanda didn't move a muscle. She didn't even breathe. She just listened, hoping that she'd imagined what she'd heard and praying with all her heart that she wouldn't hear it again.

But she did.

"Ma-maaaaaa!"

This time the sound was loud and clear as it drifted through the open window.

Amanda's heart stopped.

The doll that she'd left on the patio was crying out into the night! The doll that they'd dug up from Barnsey's yard! The doll without a voice box!

Amanda rolled over onto her stomach and buried her head under the pillow, pretending the sound was her imagination. But even with the pillow over her head, Amanda could still hear the doll crying.

"Ma-maaaaaa!"

The cry came again. This time it was so distant and muffled, Amanda barely heard it at all.

But Amanda didn't move. She just lay there listening. And listening. And listening. Until finally, the silence put her to sleep.

Amanda's head was still under the pillow when she woke up. And because that wasn't the way she usually slept, she was confused at first, wondering how she got that way. The moment she remembered, she felt herself starting to panic.

Amanda kept her head under the pillow, and listened hard, terrified that she'd hear the doll crying "Mama" again. But all she heard was the sound of birds singing outside her window. As she slowly poked her head out, she realized that morning had finally come to her rescue, because her entire room was full of the sun's light.

Still, Amanda didn't want to get out of bed. She didn't want to face what she knew she had to do.

Jarrad was wrong. The doll's voice box hadn't fallen out into the hole. The doll really was haunted! And whether he liked it or not, Jarrad was just going to have to help her get rid of it. Even if that meant digging up the dead squirrel so that they could put the haunted doll back in its grave . . . on the property that really belonged to Barnsey.

Amanda finally forced herself out of bed and over to the window in her room. There was a part of her that was afraid to even look down onto the patio. Just the idea of having to look at the haunted doll already had Amanda's nerves on end. She had no idea how she was going to find the courage to actually pick it up and bury it again.

Amanda pulled the curtains back slowly, as if she were expecting someone or something on the other side to jump out and say "boo!" And when she finally looked down onto the patio, she gasped as if someone really had. Because the sight that confronted her was just as startling.

7

Amanda couldn't believe her eyes. The doll was gone!

She ran out of her room, down the stairs, and out the back door of the house, still dressed in her pajamas. She was hoping that somehow the doll had been knocked off the table during the night. And that it was just lying on the ground somewhere she couldn't see from her bedroom window.

But even as she started to search the patio, Amanda was sure that it was hopeless. Something told her that no matter how hard she looked, she was never going to find that doll. Still, she didn't give up until she'd searched under every piece of furniture on the patio and crisscrossed the entire lawn twice.

Something very, very strange was going on. And Amanda had the awful feeling that it had something to do with Barnsey.

Amanda rushed back into the house to shower and dress quickly. She wanted to get to her friends. She wanted to tell them about the doll. She could only imagine what Kevin and Laura would say when they heard that the doll really was haunted. She was sure they would freak. And wait until she told them that the doll had disappeared, too. But what Amanda really wanted was to hear Jarrad come up with some logical explanation for what had happened. Because she certainly couldn't come up with one of her own.

Amanda stood under the spray of the shower, thinking about the doll and wondering about Barnsey. And she was getting more and more spooked by the minute. Especially when the shower curtain started to move.

One fold after the next began to sway as if someone was brushing past it on the other side.

Amanda stood frozen under the stream of hot water, terrified. Someone was in the bathroom with her.

That's impossible, Amanda told herself. She was sure she'd locked the door.

Still, she was too afraid to look. Finally, she forced herself to peek out from behind the curtain.

The bathroom was empty. Her pajamas were in a pile on the floor, just as she'd left them. And the door was indeed locked. Yet something didn't feel right. Amanda scanned the room for a few more seconds before she felt safe enough to let the shower curtain fall shut again.

She sighed as she stepped back under the spray. She could feel her shoulders start to relax the moment the hot water beat down on them. She was definitely alone, and safe.

But just as she started washing her face, Amanda heard a faint, squeaky sound coming from inside the bathroom!

Amanda thrust her face under the stream of water and wiped the soap away from her eyes as quickly as she could. Then she pulled back the curtain to look out into the bathroom again.

Her eyes were blurry, and they stung a little from the soap, but Amanda could see that the bathroom was still empty. She was still all alone.

Amanda decided that maybe that was the problem. Maybe she shouldn't be alone. Maybe she was letting herself get carried away over Barnsey and that stupid doll. She rinsed herself off quickly, and turned off the water. She dried just as quickly and wrapped the towel around herself as she stepped out of the tub.

It was then that she saw it. Amanda's whole body began to tremble with fear. There, right before her very eyes, was proof positive that Amanda hadn't been alone at all.

8

I want my baby back!

Amanda stood staring into the mirror above the sink. She didn't want to believe what she was seeing. But it was true. Someone really had been in the bathroom with her.

Suddenly, Amanda was gripped by the horrifying feeling that whoever it was might still be there, standing right behind her. Amanda spun around to look.

No one was there.

Her imagination was playing tricks on her. At least she hoped that was what was happening. Amanda wanted to believe that when she turned back around, the only thing she would see in the mirror would be her own reflection.

That wasn't the case.

I want my baby back!

Amanda blinked hard. But the words that were written in the steam that covered the mirror didn't go away.

Amanda was so frightened that she could barely breathe. The bathroom suddenly felt very hot. She had to get out of there. She reached for the doorknob and tried to turn it. But it didn't budge. She started twisting it more frantically, pulling on the door at the same time.

Suddenly, Amanda realized that the reason the door wouldn't open was because it was still locked. But that terrified her even more. Because that meant that whoever had left the message on the mirror got into the bathroom without using the door! Or maybe whoever it was that left the message didn't have to be in the bathroom at all!

There was only one person Amanda knew who had that kind of power. Barnsey!

By the time Amanda managed to get the bathroom door open, she was completely convinced that Barnsey had already put a spell on her. Her head was spinning with thoughts of all the terrible things that might happen to her.

Amanda raced into her bedroom and slammed the door shut behind her. But someone was already there, waiting for her. When Amanda bumped into a body, she started to scream.

"What's the matter with you?" Laura shouted at her.

Amanda's brain tried to send out the signal to stop her from screaming. There was no reason to scream. It was only her best friend who was in the room with her. But even though Amanda understood that, even though she stood there staring right at Laura, she could not stop the outburst of fear. Amanda didn't stop screaming until there was no air left in her lungs.

Just then, Amanda heard a knock. She screamed even louder.

"What in the world is going on in here?" Mrs. Peterson asked as she pushed open the door.

"Nothing, Mom." Amanda panted out the lie. There was no way she was going to tell her mother about Barnsey, because there was no way her mother would believe her. "Some creepy-crawly bug just crawled across my foot. That's all."

"Oh, for Pete's sake." Mrs. Peterson sighed. "With the way you were screaming, I thought you were being tortured up here. Could you try to keep it down a little? Your father's on the phone."

"Sorry, Mom." Amanda forced an apologetic smile.

Mrs. Peterson just shook her head as she stepped back into the hallway.

"There's no bug in here," Laura insisted the moment Mrs. Peterson closed the door.

"I'm not really screaming about a bug!" Amanda struggled to catch her breath. "I'm screaming about Barnsey. She was just in the bathroom with me!"

"Barnsey was in your bathroom?" Laura shrieked in horror. "Why didn't you tell your mother?"

"Because I don't know if she was really in the bathroom with me," Amanda started to explain. "But she sent me a message."

"Barnsey sent you a message in the bathroom?" Laura asked incredulously.

Amanda nodded.

"What kind of a message?" Laura wanted to know.

"I'll show you." Amanda grabbed Laura's arm and dragged her out into the hallway, toward the bathroom.

"Where are we going?" Laura tried to pull her arm free. But Amanda held tight. "You'll see."

When they got to the bathroom, Amanda pushed Laura in ahead of her. "Look!" Amanda turned Laura so that she was facing the mirror over the sink.

"At what?" Laura asked, confused.

Amanda looked into the mirror, and her heart sank. There was nothing for Laura to see but their own reflections.

The message was totally gone.

9

"Barnsey wants that doll back." Amanda was convinced that was what the message meant.

Laura sat on the edge of Amanda's bed, nodding her head in agreement.

Amanda had told Laura the whole story. She told her about the cries in the night, the missing doll, and finally the message on the mirror.

"How are we supposed to give it back when we don't even have it anymore?" Laura asked.

"We've got to find it," Amanda told her. "It's got to be out there somewhere."

But it wasn't.

"Maybe somebody took it," Laura suggested after they'd searched every inch of the yard without any luck.

"Who would have taken it?" Amanda asked hopelessly.

Laura just shrugged.

Then it came to Amanda, and she answered her own question. "My mother! That's who took it. I'll bet she threw it in the garbage."

Amanda was off and running before she even finished the sentence. She headed straight for the garbage cans that stood by the side door of the house. Sure enough, when she lifted the lid and looked inside, Amanda saw a plastic bag full of garbage.

The bag was heavy, and Amanda toppled the garbage can trying to get it out.

"I can't believe we have to dig through the garbage," Laura complained.

"Maybe we won't have to dig," Amanda said, struggling with the knot that held the bag closed. "Maybe it'll be right on top."

But they weren't that lucky. The last thing that had been thrown into that garbage bag were the remains of last night's dinner. There were chicken bones, and mashed potatoes, and peas. And Amanda was not about to stick her hands into that mess.

"We're gonna have to dump it out," she told Laura.

"Your mother will have a fit if we do that," Laura warned.

"Not if we clean it back up before she sees it." Amanda grabbed the bottom of the bag and turned it upside down.

Just then, the side door opened. "Amanda!" her mother's voice shrieked. "What are you doing?" Mrs. Peterson came outside to look at the enormous mess Amanda had just made on the walkway.

"Don't worry, Mom." Amanda tried to keep her mother calm. "We'll clean it up."

Amanda's little sister had followed their mother out of the house. "Ooooh," Robin giggled excitedly. "You're in trouble!"

Her mother ignored Robin's comment. "Why did you do this?" she asked Amanda.

"I have to find the doll," Amanda explained. "I thought you threw it away." But Amanda could already see that she'd been wrong about that. There was no doll in with the trash that was strewn on the ground at her feet.

"What doll?" Her mother was trying really hard to control her anger.

"The baby doll," Amanda answered. "The one that we dug up yesterday. I told you about it."

"I didn't throw it away," her mother assured her. "I never even saw the thing."

"I know what happened to it," Robin volunteered.

"What did you do with it, you little twerp?" Amanda demanded.

"I didn't touch it," Robin answered.

"Then where is it?" Amanda asked.

"Barnsey took it," Robin told her.

"Robin!" their mother scolded.

"Sorry," Robin groaned. "I mean Mrs. Barns."

"How do you know?" Amanda asked.

"I saw her do it," Robin said smugly.

"Robin, what on earth are you talking about?" Mrs. Peterson said, more as a reprimand than a question.

"Last night," Robin began her story, "when I was falling

asleep, I heard a baby say 'Mama.' It was really loud. And it happened over and over again. So I got up and looked out my window. And that's when I saw Mrs. Barns. She took the doll right off the picnic table. And that made the little girl cry."

"What little girl?" Amanda asked.

"I don't know." Robin shrugged. "Just some little girl. I never saw her before."

"Maybe it was the little girl Barnsey keeps locked up in her dungeon!" Laura gasped.

Amanda was thinking the very same thing. "Was the little girl all bloody and stuff, like somebody had been torturing her?" she asked Robin.

"Amanda!" her mother snapped. "What in the world is the matter with you? It's bad enough that you older kids make up terrible stories about Mrs. Barns, but I will not have Robin doing it, too. And I will not have you filling her head with horrible notions."

"Mom," Robin protested. "I'm not making it up."

"I don't want to hear any more about it," their mother said. She took Robin by the shoulders and turned her around to head into the house. "Come on," she said to Robin. "Let's go inside. And you two," she said over her shoulder, "clean up this mess."

Amanda and Laura began doing as they were told.

"Do you think Robin was telling the truth?" Laura asked as soon as Amanda's mother was out of earshot.

But Amanda didn't answer her. She was listening to something else, a sound she'd heard even before her mother went into the house.

"Shh," she whispered to Laura. "Listen."

Then Laura heard it, too.

It was the unmistakable sound of a little girl crying . . . and it was coming from Barnsey's backyard.

10

There really is a little girl!" Amanda gasped.

"Let's get out of here!" Laura urged.

Amanda would have liked to have done just that. But she couldn't run away. The crying she heard coming from the other side of the fence was so sad, she couldn't ignore it.

"We've got to do something," she told Laura. "We've got to try and help her."

"Are you crazy?" Laura shrieked. "We'll get ourselves killed."

"No, we won't," Amanda said, trying to calm her own fears as much as Laura's. "I'm not saying that we should go rushing into Barnsey's yard or anything. Let's just go back there and peek through the fence so we can see what's going on. Then we'll decide what to do next."

Without waiting for Laura to agree, Amanda headed for the back of the yard. Laura followed, just like she always did.

Amanda knew that she was lucky to have a friend like Laura, somebody who was always there to back her up. It made it easier to be brave, easier to do the right thing.

When they were halfway across the yard, the crying abruptly stopped. But Amanda kept going, with Laura right behind her. They approached the fence slowly and cautiously. After what had happened the day before, Amanda was afraid that Barnsey might just reach through the crack and grab her again. But she had to look anyway. She had to find out about the "little girl."

With Laura clinging to the back of her shirt, Amanda peeked through the fence into the gloomy and foreboding yard on the other side.

"Do you see her?" Laura whispered.

Amanda shook her head no. She didn't see anybody at all. Barnsey's backyard looked completely deserted.

Laura pushed in next to Amanda to look for herself.

"What could have happened to her?" Amanda wondered aloud. She wasn't expecting an answer from Laura. But she got one.

"Maybe Barnsey dragged her back to the dungeon."

Just then, Mrs. Barns appeared from around the side of the shed. She was all dirty, and carrying a big shovel.

"Look!" Laura practically screamed. "Barnsey buried her!"

"Shh," Amanda warned.

But it was too late. Mrs. Barns's head whirled in their direction.

Amanda gasped as Barnsey stalked toward the fence with the shovel in her hand and an angry look on her face.

Amanda and Laura started backing away. But before Amanda could turn to run, somebody grabbed her from behind.

11

Let me go!" Amanda screamed, struggling frantically against the grip that held fast around her waist.

She heard laughter close to her ear. Kevin's laughter.

"Knock it off," Jarrad told him.

Kevin released his grip, but continued laughing. He thought he was pretty funny sneaking up on Amanda and scaring her like that.

But Amanda made him stop laughing real fast. "Barnsey's after us!" she shouted.

That was all Kevin needed to hear before he was off and running way ahead of the rest of them.

"We're in big trouble," Amanda told the boys when they finally reached the patio.

"What kind of trouble?" Kevin asked.

"We just saw Barnsey bury the little girl she kept in the dungeon," Laura blurted out.

"You what?" Jarrad practically shouted.

"We saw Barnsey bury the little girl," Laura repeated.

"Was she dead or alive?" Kevin asked, wide-eyed.

"I don't know," Laura told him.

"What do you mean you don't know?" Kevin huffed. "Did you see the kid or not?"

"Well, not exactly," Amanda told him. "We heard a little girl crying in Barnsey's backyard. But when we went back there to look, there was no little girl. Just Barnsey carrying a big shovel."

"Then she buried her alive!" Kevin gasped.

Jarrad started to laugh.

"It's not funny," Laura hollered at him. "It's true!"

"Just because Barnsey had a shovel doesn't mean that she buried a little girl," Jarrad said. "Besides, you didn't even see a little girl, did you?"

"No," Amanda answered. "But we heard her."

"Robin saw her," Laura reminded Amanda.

"Robin!" Jarrad laughed even harder. "She's always making up stuff just to get attention."

"I don't think she made this up," Amanda said. "Last night, I heard the doll crying again. I didn't tell anybody about it, except Laura. But just a little while ago, Robin said that she heard the doll, too. And when she got up to look out her window, she saw Barnsey taking it. And the little girl was with her."

"That proves that there really is a little girl," Laura told the boys.

"All that proves is that Robin has a very active imagination," Jarrad disagreed.

"Wait a minute," Amanda said, more to herself than to the others. "If Barnsey took the doll last night, who left the message this morning?"

"What message?" Jarrad asked.

"Somebody wrote a message on the bathroom mirror," Amanda told him. "It said, 'I want my baby back.' At first, I thought Barnsey did it. But if Barnsey already had the doll, then somebody else must have done it."

"Maybe it was the little girl," Kevin suggested.

"The little girl that Barnsey buried?" Jarrad asked.

Kevin nodded.

"Let me ask you a question, you idiot," Jarrad said to Kevin. "If there really was a little girl that Barnsey kept locked in the dungeon, how the heck did she get out to leave a message on Amanda's mirror?"

Kevin didn't answer.

"And if she could get out of the dungeon to go write messages," Jarrad continued, "how come she didn't just break out of the dungeon and go home?"

Kevin was stumped. "Okay, maybe it wasn't the little girl."

"And maybe Barnsey didn't take the doll, either," Jarrad suggested.

"Maybe Jarrad's right," Kevin said in a tone of voice that spelled trouble. "Maybe nobody took the doll."

"What are you talking about?" Laura asked. "Somebody had to have taken that doll."

"If that doll was crying again," Kevin went on, "then it really is haunted, right?"

Amanda and Laura nodded.

"Yeah, well, maybe it's so haunted that it just walked away all by itself," Kevin told them. "Maybe it's like that Chuckie guy. You know, that maniac doll in the movies who runs around trying to kill everybody? Maybe that haunted baby doll is just hiding out here waiting to do us in!"

Amanda couldn't help scanning the yard around her, terrified for a moment that maybe Kevin was right. With all that was going on, she almost expected to see the mama-screaming baby doll running at them wielding the Chuckie doll's knife.

Laura's eyes were darting about, too.

"Did somebody kick you in the head when you were a baby, or what?" Jarrad asked Kevin, totally exasperated.

Amanda could tell that Jarrad didn't believe any of it. And she couldn't really blame him. Listening to herself and Laura was bad enough. But listening to Kevin was like a trip to a whole new dimension. It was all starting to sound pretty unbelievable, even to her.

"Maybe I'm just going nuts," Amanda said. It seemed to be the only explanation left that made any sense.

"That's exactly what happened to Todd French!" Kevin gasped. "The day he got his head split open, he was following his mother into the supermarket when he felt someone tap him on the shoulder. But when he turned around to look, there was nobody there. I mean nobody at all. But it was because Todd wasn't paying attention to where he was going that he slammed right into the door and had to be rushed to the hospital to get stitches!"

Amanda couldn't believe that Kevin had actually found a way to pin her insanity plea on Barnsey. But he had. And now that his own cuckoo train was on the fast track, there seemed to be no stopping it.

"And that's not the only time something like that has happened to him." The train was picking up steam. "Todd says that he's always seeing and hearing stuff that isn't really there. Because Barnsey's trying to drive him nuts. It's all part of the spell. And Todd's getting so desperate that he's even thinking about trying to sneak into Barnsey's house to get his cap back," Kevin informed them. "Because he's convinced that every time Barnsey rubs it, he loses another little piece of his mind! And if I were you," Kevin warned Amanda, "I'd think about doing the same thing."

"What are you talking about?" Amanda asked, sounding just as irritated as she was scared.

"Your bracelet," Kevin shot back. "Barnsey's got it. And you better figure out a way to get it back before she starts rubbing it as hard as she's been rubbing Todd French's baseball cap!"

"Oh, brother," Jarrad huffed. "Will you forget about Todd French! Barnsey is not trying to drive him nuts. Todd French is already nuts. And so are you," he told Kevin.

"Oh, I don't think so," Kevin shot back. "If anybody's nuts around here, it's you. When are you gonna give up and admit the truth about Barnsey?"

"When I see some proof with my own two eyes," Jarrad answered.

"I don't even know why I bother talking to you," Kevin said. He walked away from Jarrad, shaking his head in disgust, and made his way toward the swing set on the other side of the yard.

"There really is something strange going on," Amanda told Jarrad. "Maybe Kevin's right. Maybe all of this is happening because Barnsey really does have my bracelet. And maybe I should be trying to figure out a way to get it back."

"You've got to stop letting Kevin get to you like this," he said. "I'm telling you, Todd French does not have a spell on him. And neither do you. The best thing that you can do is nothing at all. I guarantee you that if we all just leave Barnsey alone, she'll leave us alone, too."

"This has nothing to do with Kevin," Amanda said. "I know that Todd French is just a goofball. But I'm not Todd French. I know what I heard. And I know what I saw."

"Yeah," Laura chimed in. "Somebody wrote a message in the steam on the mirror while Amanda was in the shower, and the door was locked. How do you explain that?"

"You saw the message too?" Jarrad asked Laura.

"Well, no," Laura was forced to admit. "But Amanda did."

"And I wasn't imagining it," Amanda said, trying to convince herself as much as Jarrad. "It really was there. And it was crystal clear too. It said, 'I want my baby back.'"

Just then, Kevin called to them from the other side of the yard. "Hey, Jarrad," he shouted, sounding very jittery. "You might wanna bring your own two eyes over here and take a look at this!"

"He's the only maniac running around this yard," Jarrad said as he headed for Kevin, who was standing near Robin's sandbox by the side of the swing set.

Amanda and Laura followed.

The moment they saw what Kevin was pointing to, Laura grabbed Amanda's arm. Amanda could barely hold her up, because her own legs were starting to wobble beneath her.

There, for all eyes to see, was another message, written clearly in the sand.

didn't really know what to believe. Because even if Jarrad was right, even if Kevin was responsible for the message in the sandbox, he wasn't responsible for the one on the bathroom mirror. And no matter how hard he'd tried, even Jarrad couldn't come up with a logical explanation for who was.

Amanda pulled the covers up to her chin as she glanced at the clock on the nightstand beside her bed. It was already past midnight. Amanda had been tossing and turning for over an hour trying to get to sleep. But the horrible events of the day kept playing over and over again inside her mind. And no matter how hard she tried, she couldn't seem to shut them off.

Think something happy, Amanda told herself as she rolled back over onto her stomach, fluffing the pillow under her head again. As she squeezed her eyes shut, she tried to do just that.

At first it wasn't easy. In fact, it was almost like there was a ping-pong game going on inside her head between the happy thoughts and the horrifying ones. But after a while, the happy thoughts started to win. And before she even knew what was happening, the nightmares of the

12

I *want my baby back—now!*

Amanda couldn't stop thinking about the message in the sandbox any more than she could stop thinking about the message on the mirror. And she'd been thinking about it all day.

Jarrad had claimed that the writing in the sandbox was Kevin's doing, insisting that Kevin was just trying to prove to him that something scary really was going on. And while Amanda thought that that was entirely possible, especially since Kevin had had such a hard time keeping a straight face while he denied Jarrad's accusations, Amanda didn't really know what to believe. Because even if Jarrad was right, even if Kevin was responsible for the message in the sandbox, he wasn't responsible for the one on the bathroom mirror. And no matter how hard he'd tried, even Jarrad couldn't come up with a logical explanation for who was.

Amanda pulled the covers up to her chin as she glanced at the clock on the nightstand beside her bed. It was already past midnight. Amanda had been tossing and turning for over an hour trying to get to sleep. But the horrible events of the day kept playing over and over again inside her mind. And no matter how hard she tried, she couldn't seem to shut them off.

Think something happy, Amanda told herself as she rolled back over onto her stomach, fluffing the pillow under her head again. As she squeezed her eyes shut, she tried to do just that.

At first it wasn't easy. In fact, it was almost like there was a ping-pong game going on inside her head between the happy thoughts and the horrifying ones. But after a while, the happy thoughts started to win. And before she even knew what was happening, the nightmares of the day started to dissolve, and Amanda found herself drifting off into another world. . . .

"Hush little baby, don't say a word . . ."

Amanda smiled as somewhere in the distance, the sweetest little voice started to sing her favorite lullaby.

"Mama's gonna buy you a mockingbird . . ."

Amanda kept listening to the song as she let herself fall deeper and deeper into sleep.

"And if that mockingbird won't sing . . ."

Before Amanda even realized it, she wasn't just listening anymore, she was singing right along.

"Mama's gonna buy you a diamond ring . . ."

The other voice started to fade. And as the shadowy images that were dancing through Amanda's dreams started to clear, Amanda found that she hadn't really drifted very far at all. Because she was home, sitting on the swing right outside of her house . . . singing to the most beautiful doll she'd ever seen.

Only it wasn't really Amanda's house. In fact, it was a house Amanda had never ever seen before, in a neighborhood that looked just like an old-fashioned painting.

There were cobblestone streets lined with lampposts,

the kind that used gaslight. And there were funny-looking cars, cars that Amanda had only seen once before, in a black-and-white movie her father had shown her.

And the clothes she was wearing looked just like the clothes Robin's old Raggedy Ann doll used to wear before Robin cut them up.

But the strangest thing of all was that Amanda wasn't even really Amanda anymore . . . she was just a little girl.

Only somehow, none of it seemed to matter to Amanda. Because somehow, Amanda felt like she was home. She felt safe and warm and loved. And her head really was full of wonderful, happy thoughts.

Amanda looked down at the doll she was cradling in her arms. The scent of lilacs filled the air around her.

"Anna . . ."

Amanda turned toward the sound of her mother's voice. Only she knew it wasn't really her mother's voice. And she knew her name wasn't Anna, either, but she wasn't bothered by it one bit. Amanda thought Anna was a beautiful name to be called.

"I made some lemonade for you . . ."

Amanda smiled at the sight of the woman standing at the open screen door. She was just about the same age as Amanda's real mother. And she was just as pretty, too.

"Why don't you come inside and let me pour you a glass?" the woman went on.

"Okay, Mommy," Amanda answered. Then she laid the doll down on the swing behind her and headed into the house.

Everything inside looked just as strange to Amanda as everything outside. Only somehow it seemed totally familiar to her. As she made her way into the kitchen, Amanda seemed to know exactly where everything was, including which cabinet to open to find her favorite cup.

She only stayed inside long enough to fill her cup with lemonade. Then she headed back out to share it with her doll.

But when Amanda reached the swing, the doll was nowhere to be seen. And before she even knew why, Amanda found herself in a panic.

"My baby's gone!" Amanda screamed as she dropped the cup of lemonade onto the porch. "Somebody took my baby!"

Amanda raced back toward the front door. But before she even made it halfway across the porch, she saw another little girl running across the front lawn . . . running away from the house . . . running away with her doll.

But it wasn't her doll! And it wasn't her house! And it wasn't a nice dream anymore.

"I want my baby back!" Amanda screamed again as she ran down the steps of the porch and headed across the lawn.

The other little girl kept on going.

Amanda didn't know who the other little girl was, or where she was running to. In fact, everything around Amanda started to feel a whole lot less familiar and a whole lot more frightening.

"Emily!" she screamed, suddenly knowing the other girl's name. "I want my baby back!"

But Emily didn't even turn around.

Amanda kept running. And running. And running . . . right out into the middle of a busy street.

"*Anna! No!!!!*"

Amanda wanted to stop what was about to happen

with all her heart. But it was too late. Before she could jump out of the way, Amanda felt herself being hit head-on by the biggest car she'd ever seen.

The impact was so hard and so fast it sent Amanda flying. . . .

Amanda closed her eyes as tight as she could, hoping that it would all just go away. She didn't want to be Anna anymore! She wanted to be Amanda! And she wanted to wake up!

Amanda felt herself landing . . . hard. When she forced her eyes open, she was sure that she would never wake up again. Because Amanda found herself lying at the bottom of a grave in Mrs. Barns's backyard . . . and Barnsey was standing right over her, dumping one shovelful of dirt after the next on top of her.

13

Amanda could feel herself gasping for air as she tried to struggle against the weight of the dirt that was piled on top of her. But no matter how hard she tried, she couldn't seem to move anything more than the tips of her fingers.

"Somebody help me!"

Amanda tried to scream, but the sound of her voice was so faint, it couldn't escape the walls of her grave any more than she could. Even if she screamed at the top of her lungs, no one would hear her. No. No one would ever be able to hear Amanda's cries for help from six feet under the moldy ground in the back of Barnsey's yard.

Barnsey buried her alive! Now she really was going to end up as just another scary story for Kevin to tell!

Just the thought of being compared to the Lizard kid was enough to startle Amanda right out of the grave. When she finally opened her eyes, she realized that she was lying in her own bed.

Amanda could see the sunlight in her room trying to sneak under the covers with her. Only she couldn't seem to let it in, because Amanda was having a heck of a time trying to get out.

The covers on her bed were way up over her head, and the sheets were tangled so tightly around her from all the tossing and turning she'd been doing, she really was having a hard time trying to free her hands.

She almost started to laugh at the idea that she really was buried alive—under her own blankets. But as she finally managed to wriggle one of her hands free and pull the covers from her face, she realized that the nightmare wasn't over at all.

Amanda wasn't just buried in blankets. She was buried in dolls!

Amanda's heart started to pound as she looked up at

the shelves above her bed, hoping that they had somehow fallen from the wall during the night, sending all of her dolls toppling down onto the bed. But every one of the shelves was in place. And Amanda started to panic.

There was no way in the world that the dolls had leapt from the shelves all by themselves. And it wasn't her imagination, either. Someone had been in her room! Someone had piled the dolls on top of her!

Amanda sprang from her bed, terrified that Barnsey had somehow managed to creep out of her dreams in the middle of the night and into her room.

Or maybe Barnsey sent the dolls toppling the same way she sent the message on the mirror. Maybe she was looking at Amanda right now through her evil crystal ball, laughing at how scared Amanda was. And maybe she was getting ready to rub Amanda's bracelet as hard as she could so that something even more terrible would happen.

If Barnsey really was trying to drive Amanda nuts, it was working. Amanda's head was spinning out of control.

Jarrad was wrong. They couldn't just "do nothing." If they didn't do something soon, Amanda really was going to end up like the Lizard kid. One thing was clear—Barnsey had no intention of leaving her alone.

Amanda didn't even bother to straighten up her room before she threw on some clothes and headed into the garage to grab her bike. She had to get to Jarrad's. She had to find a way to make him believe just how serious the situation really was. One way or another, he had to find a way to help her get that bracelet back from Barnsey!

Amanda jumped on her bike and headed down the driveway at full speed. The Petersons' driveway was the steepest in the neighborhood because their house stood at the top of a huge hill. In the winter, all the kids used Amanda's drive as the starting point for sled races. Not only was the driveway steep, but it let out into the street right at the top of another hill that stretched all the way down to the opposite end of the neighborhood. Which was exactly where Amanda was heading.

She hit the street at the end of the driveway faster than she ever had—so fast that she was having a hard time just trying to keep her feet on the pedals, which seemed to be turning all by themselves.

Amanda tried to squeeze the hand brakes to slow

herself down, but before she could even get a grip on them, she was heading down Mirybrook Road, hill number two. And she was picking up even more speed.

The front tire of her bike began to shake furiously as the handlebars started to wobble. Amanda couldn't even think about trying to grab the brakes now—it was taking all of her concentration just to keep the bike steady.

It was as if someone had taken ahold of the handlebars and was jerking them from side to side. Because try as she might, Amanda couldn't hold them straight.

The bike was as out of control as her entire life seemed to be. And as Amanda struggled against the fear that was rising inside her—the fear that Barnsey was somehow making this all happen—she clung on for dear life.

Because something terrible really was about to happen.

14

There was no way for Amanda to regain control of her bike. She was going to fall. Hard. And the longer she delayed it, the worse it was going to be. Because the bicycle was picking up speed with every passing second.

Amanda was going to go down on her right side. She knew that when she hit the blacktop, she was going to skid. The entire side of her body would get bruised. Her clothes would surely be torn. And her skin would be scraped to shreds. She just had to remember to keep her head up, to keep her face off the ground.

Amanda tried to let go, tried to give in to the fall. But

she couldn't. She kept fighting it, even though she knew that was a terrible mistake.

The bicycle was carrying her farther and farther away from the curb. She could hear a car coming up behind her.

Amanda didn't dare try to turn around to look, but she could tell that the car was getting closer. She had to get off that bike. It was the only way to stay out of the path of the car.

Amanda closed her eyes tight. She shifted her weight, and braced herself for the fall.

But Amanda didn't fall. It was as if someone caught her, the way her father used to catch her when she was first learning to ride a two-wheeler. Before she even realized what was happening, she felt herself being lifted off the bike. For a moment, Amanda felt as though she were floating. And when she finally opened her eyes, she had already landed on the ground, very gently.

Amanda was shocked to see that she wasn't on the blacktop where she had expected to fall. She'd landed safely on the strip of grass between the sidewalk and the curb.

But she didn't even have time to wonder how that was

possible before she was startled by the sound of a blaring horn and the screech of tires. The car that had been following her stopped just in time to miss Amanda's bicycle by inches. If Amanda had landed on the blacktop, she surely would have been killed.

It was a miracle. Not only had Amanda been saved from total disaster, she'd managed to escape without a scratch. As she pulled herself to her feet, Amanda felt very, very lucky.

Until she recognized the driver of the car that was still stopped directly in front of her.

Mrs. Barns sat in the driver's seat, staring right at Amanda.

It was Barnsey who had nearly run over Amanda. *Barnsey!* Amanda's heart began beating even more wildly than it already was. And when Barnsey reached out to open her car door, Amanda was sure that the old woman was coming to finish her off with her bare hands.

"No!" Amanda screamed. But as she turned to run, she found herself face-to-face with something even more terrifying than Mrs. Barns.

15

Every muscle in Amanda's body froze. Her brain was screaming at her to get away, but her body wouldn't move. She couldn't even blink. Her eyes were fixed on the little girl who stood directly in front of her.

The little girl smiled up at Amanda. It was a sweet smile, friendly and innocent. But that did not ease the fear that wound itself around Amanda's heart, threatening to crush it.

The little girl was not a real little girl. The little girl, who stood blocking Amanda's escape from Barnsey, was a ghost. Her clothes were bloodied and torn, and she was covered with dirt—as if she'd just climbed out of a grave.

Amanda was sure that the little girl standing in front

of her was the little girl Barnsey had locked in her dungeon! The little girl she'd buried in her backyard!

Amanda was so terrified, she didn't even hear her own screams. She didn't even realize that she *was* screaming until she noticed the little girl's reaction.

The little girl backed away from Amanda. Her smile faded into a look of confusion. Then her lower lip began to tremble as if she were about to burst into tears.

If only Amanda could have stopped screaming, she would have told the little girl not to cry. The poor little thing looked so pitiful. She was just a small child, maybe seven or eight years old. And the expression on her face just about broke Amanda's heart. There was a part of Amanda that wanted to comfort the little girl—if only she weren't a ghost!

"Amanda!" a voice called from the distance.

The ghost disappeared.

"Amanda!" It was Jarrad's voice, and it was much closer this time.

Amanda didn't turn toward the sound of his voice. She just continued to stare at the place where the little girl had been.

"Amanda." Jarrad shook her. "Are you okay?"

Amanda ignored the question and asked one of her own, one that seemed much more important. "Did you see her?"

"Who?" Jarrad asked. "Barnsey?" He gestured toward the car that had begun to move slowly down the street.

Out of the corner of her eye, Amanda saw Barnsey still watching even as she drove away. "No," Amanda answered. "Not Barnsey. The ghost!"

Jarrad didn't say a word. He just looked at Amanda like she was totally crazy. "Ghost?" he finally managed to choke out. "Did you hit your head when you fell?" Jarrad sounded really worried. "Maybe you have a concussion."

"I didn't hit my head," Amanda told him. But she decided that there was no point trying to convince him that she had seen a ghost. He would never believe her.

"From what I saw, that was a pretty bad accident," Jarrad said.

"That was no accident," Amanda declared. "Barnsey tried to kill me!"

"Barnsey did not try to kill you." Jarrad disputed the claim as forcefully as Amanda had made it. "Barnsey did everything she could to avoid hitting you. You were the one who was all over the road."

"That's because something happened to my bike," Amanda retorted. "Something really weird. It was as if somebody grabbed the handlebars and started shaking them. Really hard. And there was nothing I could do to control it."

"That *is* weird," Jarrad agreed, heading over to inspect Amanda's bike.

Amanda followed him. "Somebody else was controlling the bike. And I know who it was. Barnsey."

Jarrad just shook his head, not even looking at her, as he examined the bicycle.

"I don't care what you say, Jarrad," Amanda went on. "Kevin's right. Barnsey has put a curse on me. I'm gonna end up just like the Lizard kid."

"You are not." Jarrad laughed. "And Barnsey has not put a curse on you. Look at this." He pointed to the place where the handlebars fit into the frame of the bicycle. "You lost a nut. Your handlebars are broken. See?" He jiggled the handlebars to demonstrate. "You don't have a curse on you.

In fact, you're very, very lucky. Do you have any idea how badly you could have been hurt?"

Amanda's mind flashed back to the terrible moment when she realized that she had no control over the bike. "I thought I was dead," she admitted to Jarrad.

"Well, you're not," Jarrad reminded her. "Just a little shaken up."

Amanda was a lot shaken up. She felt her body trembling all over. And she had to fight very hard to keep from crying.

"Come on," Jarrad said. "I'll walk you home."

Amanda walked along beside Jarrad as he wheeled her bicycle back up the hill toward her house. All she could think about was what it felt like speeding down that hill. Her imagination was showing her one ugly picture after another of all the horrible things that might have happened.

"Don't think about it," Jarrad said, as if he could read her mind.

"It's pretty hard not to," Amanda told him.

"I know," he said sympathetically. "You had a real close call there. But you can't think about how bad it could have been. Just keep telling yourself how lucky you are to be okay, and you'll feel a whole lot better."

Amanda tried to take Jarrad's advice. She tried to force all the horrible thoughts out of her head. She tried not to think about what might have been. Instead, she told herself over and over that she was lucky.

The closer she got to home, the easier it was to believe that. Amanda really was beginning to feel a whole lot better . . . until she saw what was waiting for her in the driveway.

16

IF I DON'T GET MY BABY BACK, NO ONE WILL REST IN PEACE!!!!

The words were written in the driveway in big block letters. Every line of every letter had been traced over and over again in all different colors of chalk.

Amanda could feel her insides starting to tie themselves into a thousand different knots.

Who isn't going to rest in peace? Amanda wondered. *My friends and I? Or the rest of the bodies buried in Barnsey's backyard?*

Amanda felt as if she were going to throw up.

Jarrad just stood there staring at the driveway, looking almost as unnerved as Amanda.

"Tell me I'm imagining things now." Amanda's voice quivered.

Jarrad didn't answer. Instead, he reached down to touch one of the letters. "No. You're not imagining this. It's real chalk," he said as he held his finger out to show Amanda. "But how much you wanna bet that Kevin's clothes are covered in it?"

"What are you saying?" Amanda asked, even though she already knew the answer. "That Kevin wrote this message?"

"Yeah." Jarrad nodded as he wiped the pink and purple chalk from his finger onto his pants. "That's exactly what I'm saying. Kevin wrote this message, just like he wrote the message in the sandbox yesterday."

"How can you be so sure that Kevin wrote the message in the sandbox?" Amanda challenged. "He swore he didn't do it."

"Oh, please." Jarrad laughed. "That idiot was covered in sand. The only scary thing about that message was that

Kevin was actually stupid enough to sit in the sand while he wrote it."

Amanda had to laugh in spite of herself.

"Come on," Jarrad said as he started to wheel Amanda's bike up the driveway. "He's probably up there right now trying to hide all the chalk."

Amanda followed Jarrad to the top of the driveway, hoping they really would catch Kevin pink- and purple-handed. But it wasn't Kevin who came walking out of the garage with a handful of chalk.

"I told you that kid would do anything for attention," Jarrad said as he wheeled the bike toward the garage.

"Robin!" Amanda hollered at her little sister. "Did you do this?"

"Some of it," Robin answered nonchalantly.

"What do you mean, some of it?" Amanda growled.

"I mean I did some of it!" Robin snapped back.

Amanda spun Robin around by her shoulders so that she could look her straight in the face. "Did you write this or not?"

"I didn't write it," Robin said as she twisted herself out

of Amanda's grip. "I just traced it in different colors after it was all done. Doesn't it look pretty?"

Amanda ignored Robin's question. She had more important things on her mind. "Do you know who wrote the message?"

"Uh-huh." Robin nodded.

"Well, who was it?" Amanda screamed so loud that even Jarrad jumped.

"Was it Kevin?" Jarrad asked before Robin had a chance to answer.

"Oh, puke." Robin stuck her tongue out like she was gagging. "I wouldn't color with Kevin even if he had the last piece of chalk on earth!"

"Was it Barnsey?" Amanda blurted out her worst fear.

The moment she saw the look on Robin's face, she realized just how ridiculous that question was.

"Barnsey? No way." Robin rolled her eyes. "I'd rather color with Kevin."

"You see." Jarrad turned toward Amanda. "Barnsey didn't leave this message."

"Neither did Kevin," Amanda pointed out. "Robin, who wrote this?"

"Anna." Robin blurted out the answer. "Anna wrote the message."

Amanda could feel the blood draining from her face the moment she heard the name.

"Who's Anna?" Jarrad asked suspiciously.

Amanda's whole body started to shake. Anna was the name of the little girl in the dream she'd had the night before.

"The little girl," Robin answered in a huff.

Amanda grabbed Jarrad's arm to try and steady herself. "Anna is the little girl?" She could barely get the words out.

"Right." Robin nodded. "And she wants Emily to give her baby back."

"Who's Emily?" Amanda asked.

"Emily is the little girl who took Anna's baby," Robin explained.

"How do you know all this?" Amanda held her breath, waiting to hear the answer.

Robin rolled her eyes as if she'd just been asked the most stupid question in the whole world. "Anna told me." Robin sat down on the driveway to continue coloring.

"We've got problems even bigger than Barnsey!" Amanda told Jarrad.

"What are you talking about?" Jarrad sounded just as irritated as he did confused.

"Anna's the little girl!" Amanda shouted. But before she could even start to explain to Jarrad about her dream, Jarrad cut her off.

"Oh, brother," Jarrad huffed. "Anna is probably just another one of Robin's imaginary playmates who just happens to be a little girl. You know as well as I do that Robin's always making up stories about her imaginary friends. Like Zu-bi-dee-bop," Jarrad pointed out. "Remember him? Zu-bi-dee-bop the giant sea serpent that lived in her closet? Maybe we ought to ask her if Zu-bi-dee-bop was coloring with her, too."

"Zu-bi-dee-bop wasn't coloring with me!" Robin screamed at Jarrad before Amanda had a chance to. "And Anna is not imaginary! She's just dead!"

17

So the little girl is really a ghost. . . ."

Amanda nodded again. She'd been over and over this a thousand times with Laura as they sat on the curb in front of Amanda's house putting on their Rollerblades. But Laura was still having a hard time trying to take it all in.

"And her name is Anna. . . ."

"Yeah," Amanda said as she tugged at her laces. "Her name is Anna."

"Anna the ghost . . ."

Amanda started to giggle at just how silly that sounded. "Yeah," she laughed. "Anna the ghost."

Laura looked at Amanda like she really was losing all her marbles. That made Amanda giggle even more.

"What's so funny?" Laura started to catch a nervous case of the giggles, too.

Amanda knew that the situation wasn't really funny at all. But her brain was so fried and her nerves were so frayed that she just couldn't seem to control herself. "I just hope that Anna the ghost is as friendly as Casper the ghost," she told Laura.

Laura started laughing harder. "Well, she was coloring with Robin, right?"

Amanda shook her head.

"That's pretty friendly," Laura said.

"Yeah," Amanda agreed. "That's real friendly."

"And she saved your life, didn't she?" Laura asked seriously.

Amanda was pretty sure that Anna really had saved her life. It was the only thing that made any sense at all. Someone had definitely pulled her off her bike before Barnsey had a chance to run her down. And Anna the ghost was the only one who could have done it.

"Why do you think she did that?" Amanda asked as

she stood up on her skates. "Why do you think she wanted to save me from Barnsey?"

Laura thought about it for a second while she tied the last knot in her laces before getting up. "Maybe she just didn't want you to end up like her," she said sadly.

They had been over that a thousand times, too. And they'd both come to the conclusion that Anna was a ghost because Barnsey had killed her. In fact, it was Laura who pointed out to Amanda that Barnsey must have been the person driving the car in Amanda's dream. The car that struck Anna. The car that took her entire life away.

"She probably just didn't want Barnsey to kill you the same way that she killed her," Laura continued as she and Amanda started skating around the block.

For a moment, Amanda's heart ached for Anna. There was even a part of her that wished that she would see Anna again, so that she could thank her for saving her life. Anna really was a friendly ghost. Amanda was sure of it.

At least until Laura opened her mouth again. "Or maybe she just doesn't want Barnsey to kill you *yet*." Laura's whole tone changed.

"What do you mean?" Thanks to Laura, the fear was rising inside Amanda again, like a volcano.

"Well, Anna's the one who's been leaving all the messages, right?"

Amanda nodded.

"So Anna's the one that really wants that doll back."

"We already know all that," Amanda told Laura as they turned onto Park Drive.

"Yeah," Laura said. "But maybe Barnsey told her that you dug up her doll. And maybe she's really mad at you. Maybe she's so mad at you that she's gonna let Barnsey kill you right after you give her baby back!"

Amanda's head was spinning as fast as the wheels on her Rollerblades. Maybe Anna really was a bad ghost. Maybe she and Barnsey were trying to drive Amanda nuts together?

Amanda struggled with the facts as she struggled to stay on her feet. And the most blatant fact of all was that Amanda didn't even have Anna's baby anymore. And Anna knew it. Because Anna the ghost had told Robin the brat that she wanted "Emily" to give the baby back.

"I don't have her baby." Amanda told Laura what they both already knew. "Emily has her baby."

"Yeah, right," Laura said. "And who's Emily?" Laura was working herself into a frenzy, too. "Another ghost in Barnsey's dungeon?"

Just then, Amanda felt herself being thrust forward. Before she could turn around and scream at Laura for pushing her, Laura started to scream herself.

Amanda was moving down the street so fast that she felt as if she were Rollerblading on a sheet of ice.

As Laura's screams got farther and farther away, Amanda braced herself against the force that was pushing her from behind—straight toward the house that stood at 704 Shadow Lane.

18

Amanda panicked and hit the brake too hard. Her feet stopped abruptly, but the rest of her body kept moving forward. She had just enough time to put her hands out in front of her to break the fall. With all the pads she was wearing, she didn't get hurt at all.

Laura was still screaming. Amanda knew that she was trying to say something, but her voice was so hysterical, Amanda couldn't make out any words.

Amanda flipped herself over so that she was sitting on the pavement right in front of Barnsey's house. She saw immediately what it was that had Laura so upset.

Anna the ghost had reappeared. It was Anna who had pushed Amanda down the block. But why? What did Anna want from her now? And what was she going to do next?

Amanda sat perfectly still, watching for Anna's next move.

But Anna didn't move. She just stood there staring down at Amanda.

Amanda swallowed hard before she finally got up the nerve to speak. "I know you want your baby back." Her voice quivered as she talked to Anna. "But I don't have it anymore. So you've got to stop haunting me."

Anna shook her head no. As she took a step forward, Amanda skittered back across the grass.

"Look," Amanda yelped. "I don't even know who has your baby. And I certainly don't know anybody named Emily. Believe me, if I did, I would tell her to give your doll back."

Anna turned away from Amanda and walked the few feet to the mailbox that stood at the end of Mrs. Barns's driveway. She opened the door of the mailbox and removed a stack of letters. Then she moved back toward Amanda and dropped the letters right in Amanda's lap.

Then Anna spoke to Amanda for the first time. "You have to tell Emily to give my baby back," Anna insisted. "Or no one will rest in peace."

With that, Anna disappeared.

"I already told you," Amanda hollered after her, knowing it was hopeless even to try. "I don't know anybody named Emily!"

But Amanda did know somebody named Emily. As soon as she looked down at the letters in her lap, she realized who it was. Amanda flipped through the letters, not wanting to believe what she saw. Every piece of mail was addressed to Mrs. Barns. Mrs. *Emily* Barns.

Suddenly, Laura was beside Amanda. She was still screaming. "I can't believe it! I saw her! I really saw Anna the ghost! What did she say to you?"

Before Amanda could answer, the front door to Barnsey's house flew open and Barnsey had a question of her own. "What are you two doing there?" she snarled as she started toward the porch steps.

"Let's get out of here," Laura shrieked. With almost superhuman strength, she reached out and pulled Amanda to her feet.

"You have to tell Emily I want my baby back!"

Amanda wasn't sure whether she'd actually heard those words, or they were just echoing in her own head. Either way, it didn't matter. Amanda was not about to tell "Emily" anything. All she wanted to do was get out of there. Fast.

"Come on!" Laura was already moving.

Just as she was about to take off after Laura, Amanda's attention was drawn to all the letters that were strewn on the ground. Those letters were concrete proof of who Emily was, proof that Amanda wanted Jarrad to see with his own two eyes.

Amanda decided to grab one of the letters. She would return it later, after she'd shown it to Jarrad and Kevin.

But as Amanda bent down to take one, her skates went out from under her. A moment later, Amanda found herself sprawled helplessly on the ground as Barnsey stalked menacingly toward her.

19

Amanda scrambled to her feet with one of Barnsey's letters clutched tightly in her hand.

"Amanda! Look out!" Laura screamed.

Barnsey was just inches away. The cold skeletal fingers that had clamped down around Amanda's wrist were now reaching out to grab Amanda by the back of her shirt.

Without a second to spare, Amanda took off like the wind. Her legs were pumping so hard and so fast that she blew right by Laura.

"Wait up!" Laura yelled as they turned safely off of Shadow Lane.

But Amanda didn't slow down.

"She's not following us!" Laura shouted, struggling to catch up.

"I know," Amanda screamed back.

"So where are you going?" Laura asked, grabbing her side.

"Jarrad's," Amanda shouted. "Come on!"

Jarrad had taken Amanda's bike back to his house so that he and Kevin could try to fix her handlebars. As Amanda hit the end of Jarrad's driveway with the force of a tornado, she saw Jarrad and Kevin in the garage trying to do just that.

Amanda started waving the letter in the air as she raced toward them. But before she could even open her mouth, Laura, who was just a few feet behind, began spilling Amanda's guts for her.

"Anna the ghost is real!" Laura squealed as she sped up the driveway. "I saw her! With my own two eyes!"

"And you're never gonna believe who Emily is." Amanda jumped in before Laura got to tell all the good stuff. "Emily is Barnsey!"

"Whoa, whoa, whoa," Jarrad said, catching Amanda as she rolled into the garage. "What are you talking about?"

"This!" Amanda said smugly as she shoved the letter in Jarrad's face. She couldn't wait to see his reaction when he saw the name "Emily Barns" on the envelope.

"What is this supposed to be?" Jarrad asked as he studied the envelope.

"Look at it!" Amanda practically screamed.

"I am looking at it," Jarrad told her.

"And what does it say?" Amanda demanded.

"It says 'Occupant,'" Jarrad answered, sounding confused. "'704 Shadow Lane . . .'"

"Give me that thing," Amanda said as she tugged the envelope from Jarrad's hand.

It just wasn't possible! She couldn't have grabbed the only letter on the ground that didn't say "Emily" on it!

But she had.

Amanda screamed in frustration the moment she saw it. "I can't believe this!" she ranted. "This is supposed to have 'Emily Barns' written on it! This is supposed to prove to you that I am not crazy!" she yelled at Jarrad.

But the look on Jarrad's face told her that he definitely thought she was.

"I can't believe you risked your life for that," Laura told her. "Didn't you look at it first?"

"I didn't have time!" Amanda reminded her. "I just grabbed an envelope before Barnsey grabbed me!"

Kevin gasped. "You guys were looking through Barnsey's mail?"

"No!" Amanda shouted. "Anna the ghost threw it at me!" Amanda knew she wasn't explaining herself very well, but she was so upset that her mind was moving a lot faster than her tongue.

"Anna the ghost was going through Barnsey's mail?" Kevin's tongue always moved faster than his mind.

"She wasn't going through it," Amanda snapped. "She was just trying to tell me who Emily is so that she can get her baby back." Amanda's voice kept rising right along with her frustration. "And Emily is Barnsey! And Barnsey has the baby! And Anna wants it back! And if I don't get it for her, nobody's going to rest in peace!"

"What the heck is that supposed to mean?" Kevin asked. "Don't even tell me that the rest of Barnsey's dead relatives are going to be climbing out of their graves to haunt us! Because I'll pack up my stuff and move out of town."

"Anna didn't say that, did she?" Laura shrieked. Kevin's panic was contagious.

But Amanda didn't answer. There were so many emotions whirling around inside her that before she even realized what was happening, Amanda started to cry.

"Don't cry," Jarrad said, trying to comfort Amanda. "It's okay."

"It's not okay," Amanda insisted as she wiped the tears from her face. "I have to get that doll back." Amanda started to head out of the garage.

"Where are you going?" Jarrad asked, sounding concerned.

"I'm going home to take these skates off," she told him. "Then I'm going to Barnsey's. I have to ask 'Emily' to give Anna her baby back."

As Amanda headed down the driveway she was determined to do just that.

"Wait a minute," Jarrad called out as he ran up beside Amanda. "You're serious, aren't you?"

Amanda nodded. "I have to," she told him. "It's the only way to put an end to this."

"Okay," Jarrad said, looking just as concerned as he sounded. "Then we'll all go."

Amanda knew that Jarrad still wasn't buying the whole story, but she was sure grateful that he was planning to stick by her side anyway.

"Come on, you guys," Jarrad called to Kevin and Laura. "We're going to Barnsey's."

"Oh, no." Kevin panicked. "No way!"

Laura stood frozen.

"You don't have to come," Amanda told Laura, in the tone of voice that also told Laura that if she didn't come, Amanda would never forgive her.

"Come on," Laura sighed as she grabbed Kevin by the arm. "If I'm going, you're going."

"Not without protection, I'm not!" Kevin said, pulling away from Laura and grabbing one of Jarrad's baseball bats from the corner of the garage.

"Let me ask you a question, moron," Jarrad said as Kevin and Laura came up behind them. "Do you really think a wooden bat is enough to protect you from Barnsey? I mean, you're the guy who thinks Barnsey can blow people up on their own front lawns."

Kevin went pale. So did Laura.

Amanda knew that Jarrad was just trying to be funny and lighten the mood, but she went pale too.

Because something told Amanda that she was gonna need all the protection she could get.

20

T his is a very bad idea," Kevin said gravely. "Very bad."

Amanda wasn't too crazy about the idea herself. But there was nothing else to do. She had to ask "Emily" to give back the doll. Otherwise, the ghost would continue to haunt her. It was just that simple.

"Let's go," Amanda said to Jarrad as she took the first step onto Barnsey's driveway.

"We'll be right here if you need us," Laura said.

"All three of us," Kevin added, tapping his baseball bat on the ground.

Amanda wasn't counting on Kevin and Laura to be

much help. But if something bad really did happen, at least there would be witnesses.

"Are you as scared as I am?" Amanda asked Jarrad as they made their way up the driveway toward the old stone fortress that Barnsey called home.

Jarrad hesitated.

Amanda wanted Jarrad to tell her that he wasn't afraid at all, and that there was no reason for her to be afraid, either.

But Jarrad didn't lie. "I'm pretty scared," he admitted. Still he kept right on going.

As they stepped onto the front porch, Amanda saw the curtains move in one of the windows. Barnsey had been watching them.

"She knows we're here," Jarrad said.

Amanda had to fight the urge to turn and run.

"We'd better ring the doorbell before she comes out and accuses us of sneaking around out here." Jarrad looked for a doorbell. But there wasn't one.

"You have to knock," Amanda told him, pointing at the massive arched door that looked more like the entrance to a medieval prison than the door to a house.

There was a huge brass knocker on the door. It was the head of a gargoyle. As Jarrad reached out for it, Amanda was afraid that the thing might come to life and bite his hand off.

Luckily, that didn't happen. But when Jarrad struck the knocker against the door, the loud bang made Amanda jump. She could still hear the sound of the first knock echoing inside the house when Jarrad struck the door a second time.

Amanda yanked him away from the door. She didn't want either one of them standing too close when Barnsey opened it. She wasn't about to give Barnsey the chance to drag one of them inside. In fact, Amanda was beginning to think about running away again when the door finally creaked open.

"What do you want?" Barnsey demanded. She glared at them from inside the dark and gloomy house.

"Hello, Mrs. Barns," Jarrad managed to say.

Amanda could tell by the way his voice cracked that Jarrad was scared half to death. It was up to Amanda to do the talking. Besides, she already knew what she was going to say.

"Mrs. Barns," Amanda started, trying to sound as polite as she could. "We've come to ask you to give back the doll."

"Doll?" Barnsey let out a cackle. "What doll?"

"The doll that was buried in my backyard," Amanda explained.

"I don't know what you're talking about." Barnsey's eyes bored through Amanda.

"Anna's doll."

At the mention of the name "Anna," Barnsey stumbled as if she'd been punched. Her face went pale, and a small whimper escaped from her throat. Both hands went up to her mouth, as if to stop any other sound from escaping.

It looked to Amanda as if Barnsey might just faint dead away. For a moment, Amanda almost felt sorry for the old woman. "Mrs. Barns, are you okay?" she asked.

Barnsey narrowed her eyes. "What kind of cruel joke are you two trying to play?" She spat out the words.

"Mrs. Barns, this is not a joke," Jarrad told her.

"You're right about that," Barnsey snapped back. "You get off my property. Right now. Get off my property and don't come back. Because I promise you, if I ever catch you here again, I won't give you the chance to walk away."

Then Barnsey reached out to slam the door in their faces.

A flash of metal caught Amanda's eye. She only saw it for a second before the door closed. But Amanda knew exactly what it was. It was her friendship bracelet. And it was dangling from Barnsey's bony old wrist.

21

Was she wearing Todd French's baseball cap, too?"

If looks could kill, Kevin was about to fry. The look Amanda shot him was hot enough to burn right through the bushes he and Laura were still hiding behind and blow him to smithereens.

But Laura had already started a bushfire of her own.

"Who cares about Todd French," Laura hollered as she pushed Kevin out onto the sidewalk in front of her. "Barnsey's got Amanda's bracelet!"

"No duh," Kevin said as he turned around and pushed Laura back.

"Well then, stop acting like such an idiot," Laura said.

Before her fist could make contact with Kevin's gut, Jarrad stepped between them.

"Cut it out, you guys!" Jarrad grabbed the bat away from Kevin before Kevin tried to use it.

"Yeah," Laura said, reaching around Jarrad to get the last licks in. "Cut it out!" She shoved Kevin hard.

"If you weren't already doomed," Kevin told Laura, "I'd cream you but good!"

"Oh yeah?" Laura's hands went to her hips in a defiant stance. "And what's that supposed to mean?"

"Ooooooh, nothing." Kevin was clearly baiting the hook.

"Tell me!" Laura swallowed the bait.

"You're just doomed," Kevin taunted as he started reeling her in. "That's all."

Jarrad and Amanda stood staring at each other, dumbfounded. Of all the times in the world for Laura and Kevin to pick a fight, this was definitely not a good one. And it was definitely not a good place, either, given the fact that they were within earshot of Barnsey's house.

"I am not doomed," Laura huffed. "Amanda's the one who's doomed!"

Amanda's jaw dropped. "Thanks for the news flash!"

Laura shrugged apologetically as Kevin just kept on reeling. "Yeah, but you're doomed even worse," he told Laura.

"Come on, Kevin, give it a rest." Jarrad tried to cut the line.

But Laura wouldn't let it go. "No! I want him to tell me what he's saying!"

"Well, Barnsey's wearing Amanda's bracelet, right?"

Laura nodded at Kevin.

"And it's the same bracelet you're wearing," Kevin pointed out smugly.

"So!?" Laura rolled her eyes.

"Sooooooo," Kevin rolled his eyes back at her, "that makes you best friends with Barnsey!"

Laura's eyes got so wide that Amanda was sure that they were gonna pop right out of her head and bounce on the ground like a couple of ping-pong balls. And while Amanda knew that Kevin was just trying to torment Laura, he definitely had a point.

"Oh, no I'm not!" Laura yelled as she ripped her own bracelet from her wrist.

Kevin started laughing. "Oh, yes you are!"

Without another word, Laura stormed down the sidewalk until she was directly in front of Barnsey's house. Then she wound up her arm like she was about to pitch a fastball, and chucked her bracelet clear across Barnsey's front yard, onto the porch. "There you go, Barnsey," Laura screamed at the top of her lungs. "You can just be best friends with yourself!"

"Oh man." Kevin cracked up as Laura started strutting back down the sidewalk, looking prouder than a peacock. "Now she's really doomed!"

The victorious look on Laura's face started to melt the moment she saw the horrified one that was frozen across Amanda's.

"What?!" Laura asked Amanda nervously.

Amanda didn't have the heart to tell Laura that the bravest action of her entire life was also the dumbest.

But Kevin did. "I can't believe what an idiot you are," Kevin roared. "Now all Barnsey has to do is grab the stupid thing and rub it until she rubs you to death!"

Laura turned as pale as Anna the ghost.

"You should've just stayed best friends," Kevin kept needling. "Maybe then she would have kept you alive so that she could invite you to all her rat-eating parties and stuff!"

Kevin was working Laura into such a frenzy that she burst into tears. "I don't want to go to rat-eating parties!" Laura sobbed. "And I don't wanna die, either!"

"Now look what you've done, you stupid jerk!" Amanda scolded Kevin as she tried to comfort Laura.

"Everybody just calm down!" Jarrad finally snapped. "Nobody's going to any rat-eating parties! And nobody's gonna die, either! Right, Kevin?"

Jarrad's tone was a warning to Kevin to back down. Only, Kevin refused to.

"Well, I don't know about the dying part." Kevin laughed. "But since nobody's got a bracelet, I guess nobody's gonna be invited in for the rat-eating."

"That's it, pal." Jarrad started to lose his temper as Laura started to lose total control. "You're going up there to get that bracelet back," he told Kevin as he grabbed him by the shirt and started pulling him down the sidewalk.

"Oh, no I'm not!" Kevin stopped laughing as he struggled to pull away from Jarrad.

"Oh, yes you are!" Jarrad insisted as he pushed Kevin onto Barnsey's front yard. "Because if you don't go up on that porch and get Laura's bracelet," Jarrad said as he raised the bat over his shoulder, "I'm gonna use this thing for a whole lot more than protection!"

"She's the idiot who threw it up there," Kevin hollered.

"Yeah," Amanda hollered back. "Because you made her!"

"I'm not doing it," Kevin huffed at Jarrad.

"Fine," Jarrad shot back. "Then I'll just go up there and tell Barnsey that you're the one who wants to be invited in for rat heads and milk!"

Amanda started to laugh. She knew that Jarrad was just bluffing, but Kevin didn't. Before Jarrad could even step onto the grass, Kevin pushed him back.

"Okay, okay." Kevin panicked. "I'm going, okay!?"

"Then go!"

Watching Kevin scurrying across Barnsey's front lawn was a lot like watching a jackrabbit who'd just swallowed a Mexican jumping bean. He was dashing and darting, and bobbing and weaving, and leaping and landing all over the place.

"He's gonna have a nervous breakdown before he even hits the front porch," Jarrad joked as they watched Kevin binging from tree to tree, until he finally landed by the front steps of Barnsey's house.

Amanda didn't feel the least bit sorry for Kevin, even though she knew that he was terrified beyond belief. He deserved to be terrorized after what he'd done to Laura. And Amanda was glad that Kevin was finally getting a taste of his own medicine.

Until the unthinkable happened.

"Kevin, watch out!" Amanda screamed as terror and guilt tore through her heart.

But the front door of Barnsey's house was already open. As Kevin reached down to grab the bracelet, Barnsey was already reaching out to grab him.

Before Kevin even realized what was happening, Barnsey had her evil fingers wrapped tightly around the back of his T-shirt. And she wasn't letting go.

"Nooooooo!" Amanda screamed as Kevin struggled to pull himself free.

But Barnsey was pulling harder. And Amanda was sure that the old woman was going to pull him into the house for a whole lot more than a plate of rat heads and a cup of milk.

22

It happened so quickly that Amanda couldn't believe her eyes. None of them had a chance to help Kevin. Because before they could even move, Kevin had already made the great escape. With just one quick flick of the wrist, Kevin had pulled his T-shirt over his head, and was off and running like a shot. It was definitely a move even Houdini would have envied.

He didn't even bother going down the steps. He just leapt off the porch like a superhero. His legs were running before he ever hit the ground. And when he did touch down, they started moving even faster. By the time he passed his friends, he was just a blur and a gust of wind.

As Kevin vanished down the street, Barnsey disappeared back into her house with Kevin's T-shirt in hand.

"You'd better go after him," Amanda told Jarrad. "Make sure he's okay."

"And see if he got my bracelet back," Laura added.

Jarrad headed off after Kevin. "You guys go back to Amanda's," he called over his shoulder. "We'll meet you there."

But when the two girls got back to Amanda's house, it wasn't Jarrad and Kevin they found waiting for them.

Amanda was headed up the stairs toward her room, with Laura behind her, when she heard Robin talking to someone. Amanda turned around, putting a finger to her lips to tell Laura to be quiet. Then the two of them continued creeping up the stairs as soundlessly as they could.

"How about Baby Beans?" they heard Robin say. Robin's voice was coming from her own room. "She has a beanbag body. See? You can have her."

Amanda was hoping with all her heart that Robin was talking to her imaginary sea serpent friend Zoo-bi-dee-bop. But something told her that she wasn't that lucky. And she was right.

"No, thank you, Robin," another voice answered.

It was a voice Amanda had only heard once before, but she recognized it immediately.

"Who's in there with Robin?" Laura whispered, as they reached the top of the stairs.

"Anna the ghost," Amanda answered, swallowing the lump in her throat.

Laura swallowed even harder.

"This doll's pretty cool." Robin's voice came through the open doorway again. "When you feed her a bottle, she wets her pants. Want her?"

"I don't think so," Anna answered.

Amanda and Laura snuck up to the doorway and peeked inside. There was Anna, sitting on the floor in Robin's room with her back to the door. Meanwhile, Robin was digging through her toy box, tossing out one doll after another.

"You can have any one that you want," Robin told Anna. "Really."

Amanda couldn't help thinking that the reason Anna didn't want any of Robin's dolls was because they all looked worse than the one that was buried in the backyard.

But that wasn't it at all.

"I would never take one of your babies, Robin," Anna explained. "I just want my own baby back."

"So why don't you just go to Barnsey—" Robin hesitated. "I mean 'Emily,' and tell her to give it back."

Amanda watched as Robin sat down next to Anna as if she were any other playmate.

"I've tried," Anna said. "A million times. But Emily can't see me. And she can't hear me, either."

"How come?" Robin asked.

"I'm not sure," Anna answered. "I think it's because her heart won't let her."

"That's because Barnsey doesn't have a heart," Robin griped.

"Someone has to get through to her," Anna said. Then she turned toward the open door.

Before Amanda could duck back behind the wall, Anna's eyes caught hers. It was as if Anna had known all along that Amanda was there.

"Someone has to get my baby back," Anna said, staring right into Amanda's eyes. "I will not leave without her."

23

It took the rest of the day, but Amanda and her friends finally came up with a plan to get the doll back. It was a dangerous plan. Too dangerous to attempt in the daylight. They had to wait until after dark, until after everybody else—especially Barnsey—was asleep.

Amanda arranged for Laura to spend the night at her house. That way, Amanda could be sure that Laura wouldn't chicken out. Jarrad did the same thing with Kevin.

At midnight, Amanda and Laura made their way through the darkened house and snuck out the back door onto the patio. Jarrad and Kevin were already waiting for them.

Amanda took one look at Kevin and burst into laughter.

He was all dressed in black, like a cat burglar. He was even wearing a black ski mask and black gloves. But what really made him look silly were the knee-high rubber boots he was wearing. They had bright yellow soles, and were about four sizes too big for him.

"Didn't I tell you that you looked stupid," Jarrad said to Kevin.

But Kevin just shrugged it off. "Hey, if I'm gonna be sneaking into Barnsey's backyard, I want to make sure that nobody sees me doing it."

"Then you probably ought to get rid of those boots," Amanda suggested. "They practically glow in the dark."

"No way," Kevin told her. "I'm wearing the boots in case I step on a rat or something."

Laura gasped.

"There are no rats in Barnsey's yard," Amanda assured her. "I was back there. Remember? And I didn't see a single rat."

"It's not rats we have to worry about," Jarrad reminded them. "It's Barnsey. If she catches us, we're dead."

"She's not gonna catch us," Amanda said. "Look. All

the lights are out in her house. She's probably sound asleep. We just have to be really quiet so that she stays asleep until we find that doll."

"What if we don't find it?" Kevin asked.

"We will find it," Amanda insisted. "How many times do I have to tell you? Barnsey buried that doll behind her shed. I'm sure of it."

"Yeah," Kevin said sarcastically. "And yesterday you were sure that it was the 'little girl' she was burying back there."

"That was before we knew that the 'little girl' was a ghost," Laura told him. "Barnsey was burying the doll," Laura said, agreeing with Amanda. "That's what made Anna cry."

"You'd better hope that's what happened," Jarrad said. "Because if Barnsey didn't really bury the doll, if she brought it inside her house, we're never getting it back."

Amanda knew that was true. Even the thought of being haunted by a yard full of ghosts for the rest of her life was not enough to make Amanda risk breaking into Barnsey's house. Not without a SWAT team, anyway. "She buried it," Amanda said, more to herself than to her friends.

"Then let's get this over with," Jarrad said. He started across the lawn, carrying the same shovel that he'd used the first time they dug up the doll.

Amanda followed with Laura hanging on to her shirt. Kevin brought up the rear, clomping along in his oversized boots.

"Now remember." Jarrad began whispering instructions. "Let's stay close together. And no talking unless it is absolutely necessary. Kevin and I will watch the ground to try and spot where Barnsey was digging. Amanda and Laura, you watch our backs."

"Let's just hope nobody's back there digging already," Kevin said, "from under the earth."

They all exchanged looks.

"Do you have the flashlight?" Jarrad finally asked Kevin.

"Right here," Kevin answered. Then he turned it on and flashed it right in Jarrad's face.

Jarrad's hand shot out and grabbed Kevin's arm. "Keep that thing pointed down at the ground, you moron," Jarrad whisper-hollered.

Then they continued on in silence. The closer they

got to the fence, the slower they seemed to be walking. But they got there anyway.

"I'll go in first," Jarrad whispered before any of them had a chance to have second thoughts. "Kevin, you follow me. Then Laura. Then Amanda."

Amanda knew why Jarrad put her last. He wanted to make sure that neither Kevin nor Laura ran away.

"Be careful," Amanda whispered as Jarrad slipped through the slats and disappeared into Barnsey's yard. "Go," she said to Kevin.

"I don't know why I let you guys talk me into this," he complained. But he followed Jarrad through the gap in the fence anyway.

Amanda had to push Laura through. Then she turned and took one last look at her own yard, and her house. "Please don't let Barnsey catch us," she wished in a whisper. Then she slipped through the fence to join her friends.

As soon as Jarrad saw that they were all there, he began moving slowly toward the shed. The rest of them followed close behind. Jarrad had told them to stay close together, but Kevin was carrying it too far. The only way he could have gotten closer to Jarrad was if he climbed into his pocket. Jarrad kept swatting at him because Kevin kept stepping on the backs of Jarrad's sneakers with his big, clunky boots.

Kevin kept his flashlight focused on the ground so they could see where they were going. Amanda realized that that was where her eyes were focused as well. But she wasn't supposed to be watching the ground. She was supposed to be looking out for Barnsey.

Amanda peered into the darkness toward the old stone house. The lights were still out. Barnsey had to be asleep. But Amanda stayed alert. Her eyes had adjusted to the darkness, and she kept careful watch around them as they moved toward the back of the shed.

Amanda stumbled as her foot sank into very soft ground—ground that had recently been turned over. For a moment, she was terrified that there really was a body beneath her, digging its way out. But she didn't have a chance to tell the others. Because Amanda's whispers were drowned out by a louder, more insistent sound.

"Ma-maaaa!"

24

The cry that rose from the grave beneath Amanda tore through the earth and echoed through the darkness that surrounded them. And for a split second, Amanda had to remind herself that the sound was actually coming from a doll. Because the voice was so loud and so clear that it sounded just like the desperate cries of a lost child calling out for its mother.

Amanda stepped back off the grave, feeling awfully relieved that they had finally found the spot. "She's under there," Amanda said, pointing to the ground in front of her as she waited for Jarrad to start digging.

But Jarrad didn't move. Neither did Kevin or Laura.

They just stood there frozen like a goofy group of horrified-looking mannequins.

"Come on, Jarrad." Amanda tugged at Jarrad's shirt to try and snap him out of his daze. "Dig her up, so that we can get out of here!"

It took a second before Jarrad was able to speak, but when he finally did, Amanda couldn't believe her ears.

"Maybe we should just get out of here period!"

Amanda would have expected to hear those words from Kevin's mouth, not Jarrad's. But the voice of reason was starting to crumble with fear.

"Maybe we shouldn't be messin' around with that thing at all." Jarrad's voice continued to crack as he pointed to the ground. "Who knows what'll happen! I mean, use your head, Amanda," Jarrad said as forcefully as his jittery tone would allow. "That doll is really haunted!"

That was not exactly the news flash of the century. "I know the doll is haunted!" Amanda shouted at Jarrad a whole lot louder than she was planning to. "I've been telling you that since the very first day we dug her up! But I guess you had to hear her crying again with your own two ears before you would really believe me!"

"Shut up!" Kevin screamed at the top of his lungs as he swung the flashlight around toward Barnsey's house. "Barnsey's gonna hear us! And then we're all gonna end up buried in a hole with that heebie-jeebie mama screaming Chuckie doll!"

"Yeah, well, if you don't stop shining that thing in Barnsey's windows, she's gonna see us, too!" Laura hollered just as loudly as she tried to grab the flashlight from Kevin. "Give me that thing!"

"No!" Kevin yelled back. "I'm in charge of the flashlight!"

"Not anymore, you're not!" Laura kept struggling to pry the thing from Kevin's hands. As she did, the beam of light crisscrossed the sky above them as if to announce the grand opening of Barnsey's backyard.

The secret mission was definitely becoming less and less of a secret. In fact, the four of them were causing enough of a commotion to wake the dead.

"If you wanted to be the flashlight guy"—Kevin yanked the flashlight from Laura's grip—"you should have said so from the beginning!"

"No!" Amanda hollered. She'd had just about enough.

"I'm gonna be the flashlight guy!" She grabbed the flashlight away from Kevin before Kevin saw it coming. "And you're gonna shut up!" She shined the light right in Kevin's face. "And you're gonna shut up, too!" She moved the flashlight so that it was shining in Laura's face. "And you." Amanda spun around so that she could point the flashlight in Jarrad's direction. "You're gonna dig!"

But before the beam of light could find its way to Jarrad, another face was illuminated as Anna the ghost materialized out of thin air.

"And what's she gonna do?"

As usual, Kevin's mouth was working a whole lot quicker than his brain. Amanda couldn't believe that he was still so mad at losing charge of the flashlight that the sight of Anna wasn't quite registering the right way.

"Well, she can't dig," Laura shot back, just as mad. "She's way too little!"

"Not to mention the fact that she's a ghost!" Jarrad's voice exploded into hysterics.

Anna the ghost was registering quite nicely in Jarrad's brain. Amanda only wished she had a camera to capture the terrified look on his face, now that he was seeing it all with his own two eyes.

The moment the information got through the dense skull that surrounded the pea that Kevin called a brain, he started to scream like he was taking a drop on the biggest roller coaster in the entire world.

"Stop screaming!" Amanda tried to shut him up. "You're gonna scare her!"

"*I'm* gonna scare *her?!*" Kevin got the words out with the last little bit of air that burst through his lips before he sucked in some more and started screaming all over again.

Before Amanda could even try to calm everyone down, including Anna, the shadow of someone else was looming over them.

25

As Barnsey stepped into the spotlight, terror tore through Amanda's chest like a poisonous arrow.

Amanda was trembling so badly that she had to use both hands to try and steady the flashlight. She really wanted to just drop the stupid thing and run. But she wasn't about to leave her friends behind. And she wasn't about to let Barnsey slip out of the spotlight and back into darkness where she could attack them by surprise. If anyone was gonna get the chance to make some fast moves, Amanda wanted to make sure that it was going to be them.

For a second, everyone, including Anna, stood perfectly still. Even Kevin stopped screaming his head off over Anna's appearance the moment he saw Barnsey. His mouth hung wide open.

Barnsey herself stood frozen. Her small, bony body was trembling as violently as Amanda's as she stood there glaring at them. But Barnsey wasn't shaking with fear, she was shaking with rage.

"Don't move." Barnsey's voice crackled through the air. "Don't even breathe. Or I promise you will never live to see the light of day!"

That was all the four of them needed to hear to spring into action.

In one quick, not-so-easy maneuver, Kevin was out of his oversized glow-in-the-dark boots and running full speed toward the fence. Jarrad was so close behind, he was practically in *Kevin's* back pocket, and Laura was right behind them.

As Barnsey took a step forward, Amanda finally lowered the flashlight. It was definitely time to just drop the stupid thing and run!

26

As Amanda took her first step, Anna started to cry. It was a soft, muffled sound. But it was so full of sadness that Amanda couldn't hear anything else.

Amanda's head told her to keep moving. But her heart wouldn't let her. She couldn't leave that poor little girl crying alone in the night, even if the little girl happened to be a ghost. Amanda stopped running for her own life, and turned back toward Anna.

Anna was standing between Amanda and Barnsey. "Emily," Anna sobbed. "Emily, please. You have to look at me."

"What are you doing here?" Barnsey raged. "Why do you keep tormenting me?"

For a moment, Amanda thought that Barnsey was talking to Anna. But she wasn't. Barnsey was looking right past Anna, glaring at Amanda, waiting for an answer.

Amanda was too terrified to speak. Barnsey really couldn't see Anna. And she couldn't hear her, either. Or if she could, she was really good at pretending not to.

Amanda could hear her friends screaming at her to run, but Anna's cries kept her right where she was.

"Emily," Anna wailed. She reached out to touch her. "Please! Please! Give my baby back!"

Suddenly, Barnsey's expression changed. She wasn't looking at Amanda anymore. She wasn't focused on anything, really. Instead, Barnsey had a faraway look in her eye, as if she were daydreaming about something. It looked to Amanda as if Barnsey were about to cry.

"Emily, please," Anna pleaded. "You have to look at me."

Suddenly, Barnsey's forehead crinkled into it's usual

scowl. As she snapped out of her daze, she wasn't looking at Anna at all. She was glaring at Amanda.

"I warned you what would happen if I ever caught you on my property again," Barnsey snarled at Amanda.

Then she took a step forward—and walked right through Anna the ghost.

27

Y ou'd better run while you still have the chance," Barnsey warned as she stalked toward Amanda.

But Amanda held her ground. There was no way she was abandoning Anna. "No," she told Barnsey defiantly. "I'm not leaving until you give back Anna's doll."

That stopped Barnsey dead in her tracks. "You want that doll?" she yelled at Amanda. "Fine."

The old woman picked up the shovel that Jarrad had dropped and started to dig.

"I'll be happy to get rid of this doll," Barnsey ranted. She wasn't really talking to Amanda. She was just rambling to herself, like a crazy person. "I wish I'd never taken it in the first place. The day I took this doll was the worst day of my life. And I have spent every day for the past sixty-five years regretting it."

Barnsey stopped digging and bent down to pull the doll from its grave. "Here," she shouted at Amanda. "You take it!"

Barnsey was just about to throw the doll at Amanda when something stopped her.

"Emily." Anna's voice was gentle and pleading. "Please give her back to me."

Barnsey closed her eyes tightly. And when she opened them again, she wasn't looking at Amanda. She was looking straight at Anna, who was standing right in front of her.

"Anna," Barnsey managed to say before she burst into tears. "Oh, Anna, is it really you?"

"Yes, Emily." Anna smiled. "It's really me."

Then Barnsey knelt down in front of the little girl so that they were face-to-face. "Oh, Anna," she cried. "I'm so sorry. I'm sorry I took your doll. I only wanted to play with her for a little while. I would have given her back.

Only I never got the chance." Barnsey's whole body shook as she began to cry even harder.

Amanda could feel tears welling up in her own eyes as she watched the scene.

"I never meant for anything bad to happen," Barnsey went on. "When I saw that car coming, I hollered for you to stop. But it was already too late."

Amanda flashed back to her dream. She saw Emily running down the street with the doll. She saw the car. Then she heard the scream, "Anna, no!" It was Emily's voice she'd heard. Emily had tried to stop her.

"I would give anything to be able to change what happened to you, Anna," Emily said.

"You can't change the past, Emily," Anna told her. "No one can. But you can give my baby back to me."

Emily picked up the doll that was resting on her lap and offered it to Anna.

The instant Anna took the doll, it began to change. In Anna's arms, the doll became beautiful. Her blue eyes sparkled. Her hair looked like silk. And her dress seemed brand-new.

"*Ma-ma.*" This time it wasn't a cry, but a contented murmur.

Anna hugged her baby close and smiled. Then Anna began to change, too. She wasn't a sad little ghost anymore. She was the most beautiful little girl Amanda had ever seen.

"Thank you, Emily," Anna said happily. "And thank you, too, Amanda."

"I'm so glad you got your baby back," Amanda answered.

"Now I can rest in peace," Anna sighed. "Now everyone can rest."

With that, Anna disappeared.

Barnsey was still kneeling on the ground. She had her face in her hand and was crying as if she would never stop.

Amanda walked over to Barnsey and knelt down beside her. "Don't cry, Mrs. Barns," Amanda said soothingly, trying to hold back her own tears. She put a hand on Mrs. Barns's shoulder. "It's okay," she told her.

Barnsey looked up at Amanda. Then she wrapped her arms around her in a tight embrace, accepting her comfort.

"It's okay," Amanda repeated, holding on to Barnsey just as tightly.

From somewhere off in the distance, Anna's voice echoed that sentiment. *"Don't cry, Emily. It is okay. It's all okay now."*

28

"Hey Barnsey," Kevin hollered as he squeezed through the gap in the fence. "Show 'em what you got in your pockets!"

Barnsey smiled devilishly as she reached into the front of her oversized "grave-digging smock," and pulled out a bloody red, slimy, slithery, squiggly, squirmy disgusting-looking rat by its tail.

"Oh man," Jarrad groaned. "That's so gross!"

"*Ewwwwwww!*" Laura turned away, crinkling her nose up in disgust.

"Now show them how you eat it," Kevin ordered as he

stepped back into Amanda's yard, carrying Barnsey's grave-digging shovel.

Barnsey started to giggle as she lifted the rat to her mouth.

"You're not really gonna do it, are you?" Jarrad asked, cringing at the sight.

Barnsey didn't even answer before she sank her teeth into the rat's neck and bit off its entire head.

Kevin cracked up as he and Barnsey gave each other the high-five. "I told you she loves rats!"

Barnsey winked at Amanda, then handed the rest of the gummy rat to Kevin, who immediately ripped off the tail and popped it into his mouth.

"She likes the gummy worms, too," Kevin informed the group. "But the rats are her favorite."

"Only the heads, though," Barnsey reminded him.

"Yeah," Kevin laughed. "Only the heads."

"There's something seriously wrong with the two of you," Jarrad said as he grabbed the shovel away from Kevin.

"Hey! I'm in charge of the grave-digging shovel!" Kevin yelled as he pulled it back from Jarrad. "Tell him, Barnsey."

In her wildest dreams, Amanda would have never imagined the scene that was taking place around her. As she stood there in her own backyard, surrounded by her very best friends on earth, she smiled up toward the sky, hoping that Anna was somehow watching the scene as well. Because with all of her heart, Amanda was truly grateful to Anna the ghost, for bringing a new friend into their lives.

Amanda's parents had been right about Mrs. Barns. She really was just a lonely old lady, who didn't have any family or friends—and not because they were buried in her backyard, either. Mrs. Barns explained to Amanda, and the others, that because she'd never gotten married, she didn't have any children of her own. And because most of her friends lived out of town, it was hard for them to visit.

So, Emily Barns wasn't an evil old witch. She was actually a cool, funny, *nice* little old lady. She was probably the only grown-up in the whole neighborhood that could tolerate Kevin.

It all started the day after Emily gave Anna her baby back. It was almost as if Barnsey herself had been living under a spell, because when Anna finally found a way to break it, Emily Barns had become a whole new person.

She gave back Amanda's friendship bracelet, all shiny and polished. And Laura's, too. And she gave back Kevin's glow-in-the-dark boots, along with a smaller pair she had bought him that actually fit. And, when she gave back his T-shirt, it was all cleaned and pressed, with a name tag she'd sewn in herself.

In fact, kids all over the neighborhood were getting their stuff back. Including Todd French, who was still the only kid around that Barnsey *couldn't* tolerate. She thought he was a real goofball. And Kevin had to agree. Especially when Todd fell down the sewer three days after he got his baseball cap back and six emergency trucks had to come get him out.

As the weeks went by, Barnsey did everything she could to dispel the terrible rumors that had followed her ever since Anna had died. She even started giving tours of her "dungeon," which wasn't a dungeon at all—just a regular old basement. That was a truly depressing tour for Kevin, who still wanted to believe that Barnsey was bigger than life. Barnsey promised to set up her basement like a real dungeon for Halloween, just to keep Kevin happy.

The only thing left that no one seemed to be able to

explain was the "Lizard kid." Emily had never even heard of him. But she really liked hearing Kevin tell her the story . . . over and over again.

Funny how rumors always start and end in the very same place, Amanda thought as she stood watching her friends.

"Hand over the grave-digging shovel," Barnsey told Kevin.

It wasn't really a "grave-digging" shovel. It was just a regular garden shovel. And Barnsey wasn't wearing a "grave-digging smock" either. Just an apron. But Kevin still loved to tease Emily, even though he couldn't bring himself to call her that. No. Kevin still fondly referred to Emily as "Barnsey," and she didn't seem to mind it one bit.

"You know, Barnsey." Kevin was irritated by the fact that he'd lost charge of the shovel. "You're gonna have to dig a hole as big as a grave to plant that thing. You might have a heart attack or something."

"Ke-vin!" Laura scolded.

Emily laughed. "Don't you worry about it," she told Kevin. "I've been digging holes long before you were ever born."

"Ain't that the truth," Kevin shot back.

Emily laughed even harder.

"So what am I supposed to be in charge of?" Kevin huffed.

"Supervising." Emily smiled. "Besides, it was my idea to plant it," she pointed out smugly. "So I get to dig." And with that, Emily pitched the shovel into the dirt right on top of the spot where they'd found Anna's doll.

It really was Emily's idea. Even though all four of them had gone to the nursery with her to pick it out. And all five of them had agreed upon it the moment they saw it. It was a rosebush, with beautiful pink little roses that were already in bloom. It was the perfect thing for them to plant in memory of Anna. And Emily said that if they planted it in the very same spot where they'd found Anna's baby, it would always remind them of how they all came together.

"Barnsey's got a better arm than you do," Kevin told Jarrad as Emily pitched one shovelful of dirt after the next over her shoulder.

"How much deeper do we have to go?" Laura asked Emily as she and Amanda looked on.

"Just a little deeper," Emily answered. "We need to make lots of soft dirt so the roots can breathe."

But as Emily drove the shovel back into the ground, the shovel hit something that was anything but soft.

"Hmmm," Emily said as she leaned over to see what was stopping the shovel.

"It's probably a rock," Jarrad told her as she started to push away the dirt.

"It better be a rock," Kevin said, joking around. "And not a relative or something!"

But Amanda couldn't help feeling a little uneasy when Emily dug into the earth again. *What was buried under there now?* she wondered.

A tinny, hard, clanking sound filled the air as Emily pushed the shovel down again.

"Oh, good heavens!" Emily knelt down and started to uncover something with her fingers. "Will you look at this?"

"What is it?" Kevin asked. "A body?"

"No." Emily giggled as she lifted an ancient, rusted jack-in-the-box from the hole she had dug.

For a moment, Amanda thought she saw a glimmer of

the old, scary Barnsey. "What is that?" she asked nervously.

"Nothing to worry about," Barnsey assured them. "Let's just say we've uncovered another ghost from the past. . . ."

Don't miss the next spine-tingling book
in the DEADTIME STORIES™ series

THE WITCHING GAME

"Aaaaggghhhh!"

Lindsey Jordan was dead. Dead, dead, dead! And she knew it. There was no place to run and no place to hide. In fact, if Lindsey hadn't tried to escape the horror in the first place, none of this would have happened. But now the horror was running loose through the house—along with a friend. And Lindsey was no longer locked inside the safety of her own room.

"Oh, man!" Lindsey's friend Bree Daniels gasped when Lindsey finally stopped screaming. "Your mother's going to kill us if she sees this mess! We'd better clean it up. And fast."

"No way," Lindsey snarled. "We didn't make this mess, so we're not going to clean it up." She stormed out of the living room into the foyer. Then she screamed up to the horror at the top of the stairs. "Alyssa!" she yelled at the top of her lungs. "Get down here right this minute, you little beast! And bring your sticky friend with you!"

Lindsey was answered by the sound of four little feet racing across the hallway upstairs.

"Alyssa, I'm not fooling around," Lindsey hollered. "If you don't get your butt down here right now, I'm going to come up there and kick it!"

"Drop dead!" Alyssa screamed back. Then a door slammed upstairs.

"That's it," Lindsey huffed as she took the first step. "I've had it with that kid. I'm going to kill her."

Bree grabbed Lindsey's arm to stop her. "We don't have time to kill her. Your parents will be home any minute. And if they see that living room, they're going to blame us."

Bree had a point. After all, she and Lindsey were supposed to be in charge. Lindsey had sworn to her parents that she and Bree were mature enough to be left alone with a couple of seven-year-olds. Little did they know that it would take a SWAT team to keep those brats under control.

"Don't you remember what your mother said?" Bree went on. "Watching them does not mean just being in the house. It means *watching* them."

To be honest, they hadn't been doing much watching at all. In fact, Lindsey and Bree had spent the entire afternoon locked up in Lindsey's room trying to escape the little horror and her friend. Lindsey needed the peace and quiet. Bree was helping her rehearse for the play tryouts the next day at school. They got so caught up in it that they actually managed to ignore the sounds coming from downstairs: the blaring TV, the screaming and giggling, the thumps and bumps, even the crashes.

They had forgotten all about the little horror and her partner in crime, Stephanie. That was a big mistake. Alyssa and Stephanie had turned the living room into a giant disaster area. Furniture was tipped over. The cushions were off the sofa and chairs. And what looked like every blanket in the house was draped across the mess to create a room-sized tent.

"This is unbelievable," Lindsey groaned as she and Bree walked back into the living room.

"It's not really that bad," Bree lied. "All we've got to do is fold up the blankets and fix up the furniture."

But they soon found out that that *wasn't* all they had to do.

Under the blankets, inside the tent, 128 crayons were scattered across the floor, along with every piece of every board game in the house. Stickers were stuck on everything—except the two dozen sticker books that littered the room. And in the center of it all, Alyssa's dolls were having a beach party—in a pile of sand art.

Somehow, Lindsey and Bree managed to clean the mess up. And they did it in record time. So what if the marbles from Hungry, Hungry Hippos were in the Monopoly box and Barbie's and Crystal's heads were in the trunk of the Dream Mobile? The room looked almost the way it had when Lindsey's parents left, and that was the important thing.

Bree heaved a sigh of relief as she turned off the vacuum. "I can't believe we got it all cleaned up before your parents got home."

"Yeah," Lindsey agreed. "And we've still got time to kill Alyssa." She headed into the foyer again. But before she turned to go up the stairs, she noticed something she'd missed before. The mirror on the wall across from the stairs was smeared with globs of peanut butter and jelly. "Look at this," she said to Bree in disgust. "No wonder that Stephanie kid is always so sticky."

"Do you want me to go get the glass cleaner?" Bree asked, exhausted.

"No," Lindsey answered, taking the steps two at a time. "We'll clean it up after those two little urchins are dead."

Lindsey was about to scream out to let Alyssa and her friend know what they were in for, but then she thought better of it. Why give them any warning? This would be a surprise attack.

"Shh," she whispered to Bree as they reached the top of the stairs.

They crept down the hallway toward Alyssa's room, checking to make sure that all the other rooms were still intact. They paused at Alyssa's doorway and then burst through like a couple of TV cops about to make a bust.

But the little horror was nowhere to be found.

"Where the heck did they go?" Bree said. "And what destructive thing are they doing now?"

Lindsey raced back out into the hallway in a panic. As she was trying to decide where to look first, the sound of little voices caught her attention. The sound was coming from the room across the hallway—her parents' room. She gestured for Bree to follow her.

Luckily, the bedroom was in order. But it appeared to be empty—until more chattering led Lindsey straight to her parents' bathroom door. "They're in there," she whispered to Bree, pointing at the closed door.

"What are they doing?" Bree whispered back.

Before Lindsey could even venture a guess, Alyssa herself answered the question.

"Okay, I'm going to light the candle now." Her voice drifted through the door. "Then we'll turn out the light and say the chant."

"She's got matches in there!" Bree gasped, reaching for the doorknob.

Lindsey put a hand out to stop her. "They're playing Bloody Mary," she whispered to Bree. "Let's scare the living daylights out of them."

Inside the bathroom, Alyssa was explaining the rules of the game to Stephanie. "Now we have to stare at the mirror really hard, and watch carefully for Bloody Mary. Once we say the chant, she'll appear. But only for a second. As soon as she appears, I'll make the wish. Then Bloody Mary will make it come true. Ready?"

Lindsey heard the click that told her the bathroom lights were out. There were no windows in her parents' bathroom, so Lindsey knew it was dark inside. She could just picture Alyssa and Stephanie staring through the eerie glow of candlelight into the mirror above the sink. She and Bree smiled at one another as they heard the quivering voices begin the chant:

Bloody Mary is your name.
Please appear and play this game.
For the wish we ask of you,
You must make it now come true.
Once the wish has been revealed,
Can't turn back, its fate is sealed.
In return for what you give,
We will let your spirit live.

Lindsey and Bree paused for a second, imagining the two little urchins peering into the mirror expectantly. Then the older girls let out bloodcurdling screams. Before Lindsey and Bree had even stopped screaming, Alyssa and her friend began to wail inside the bathroom. Along with their cries came fumbling and bumping sounds. The doorknob turned, but Lindsey grabbed it and held the door shut.

Alyssa and Stephanie started pounding on the door. "Help us!" they screamed. "Somebody, help us!"

Lindsey and Bree were practically doubled over with laughter.

Finally, Lindsey let go of the doorknob and the door flew wide open, sending Alyssa and Stephanie toppling over each other onto the floor.

Lindsey had gotten her revenge. And she was feeling pretty pleased with herself.

Until she caught sight of the horrifying face in the mirror.

ABOUT THE AUTHORS

As sisters, Annette and Gina Cascone share the same last name. As writers, they sometimes share the same brain. As children, they found it difficult to share anything at all.

The Cascone sisters grew up in Lawrenceville, New Jersey. It was there that Annette and Gina began making up stories. Since their father was a criminal attorney, and their mother claimed to have ESP, the Cascone sisters honed their storytelling skills early on in life—mainly to stay out of trouble.

These days, they're telling their crazy stories to anyone who will listen.

Here are the stats: Gina is older; Annette is not. Gina

is married; Annette should be. Gina has two children; Annette borrowed one. Gina has a granddaughter; Annette has a grandniece. Gina has cats; Annette has dogs. They both have a sister named Elise.

You can visit Annette and Gina at www.agcascone.com.